W9-BNW-583

EYEWITNESS BOOKS

NORTH AMERICAN INDIAN

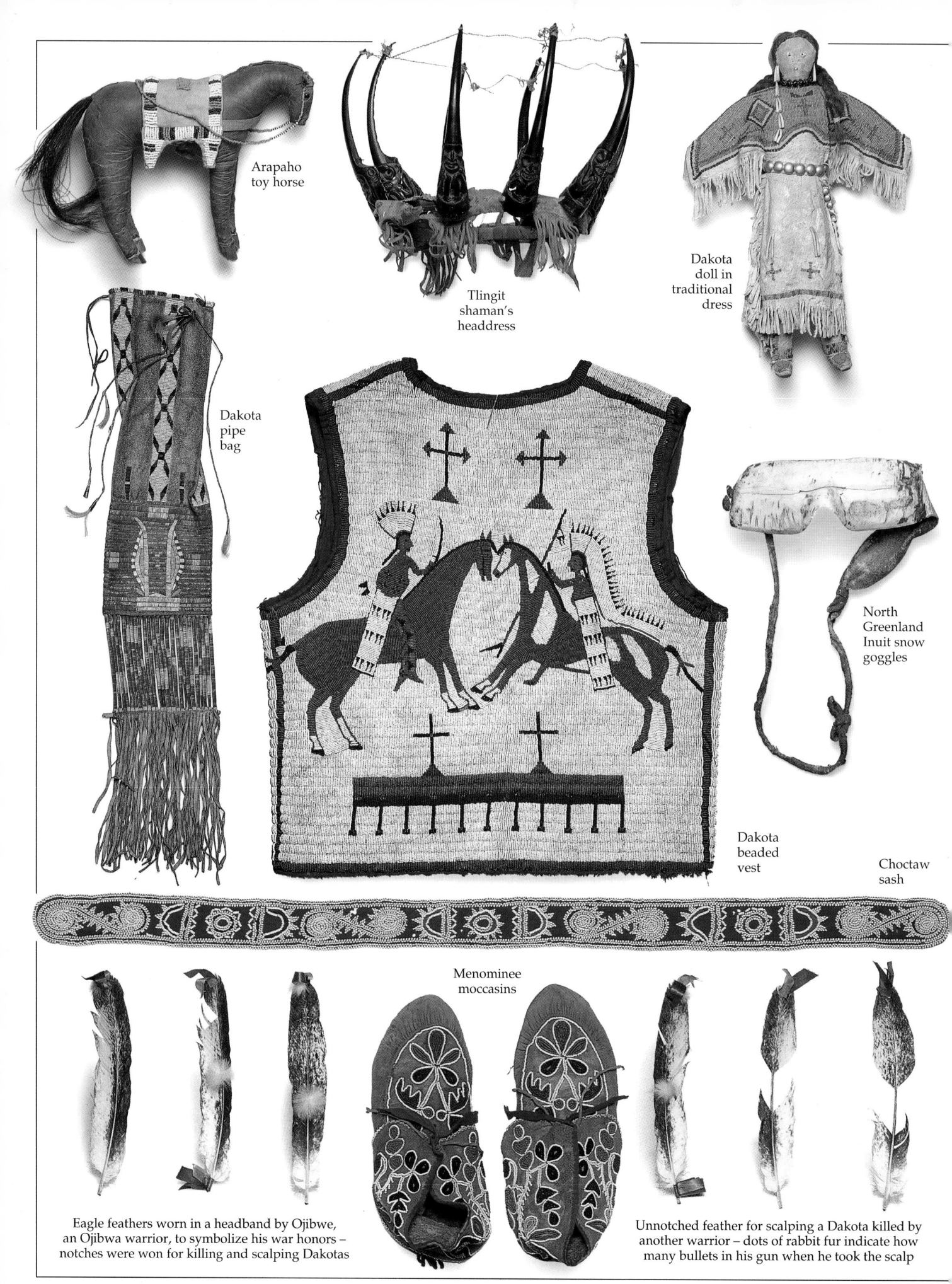
Arapaho toy horse
Tlingit shaman's headdress
Dakota doll in traditional dress
Dakota pipe bag
Dakota beaded vest
North Greenland Inuit snow goggles
Choctaw sash
Menominee moccasins
Eagle feathers worn in a headband by Ojibwe, an Ojibwa warrior, to symbolize his war honors – notches were won for killing and scalping Dakotas
Unnotched feather for scalping a Dakota killed by another warrior – dots of rabbit fur indicate how many bullets in his gun when he took the scalp

Winnebago roach headdress

Tlingit hair ornament made from pig's tusk

EYEWITNESS BOOKS

NORTH AMERICAN INDIAN

Written by
DAVID MURDOCH

Chief Consultant
STANLEY A. FREED, PhD
Curator, Department of Anthropology, A.M.N.H.

Photographed by
LYNTON GARDINER

Pair of Omaha calumets

ALFRED A. KNOPF • NEW YORK
In association with
THE AMERICAN MUSEUM OF NATURAL HISTORY

Arapaho Ghost Dance club

Penobscot stone club

Dakota whistle

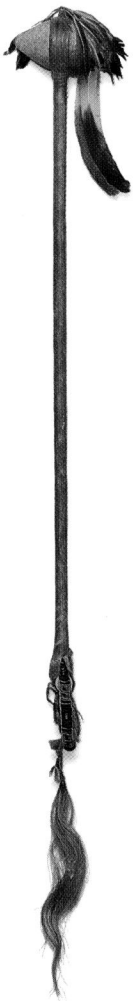

Dakota war club

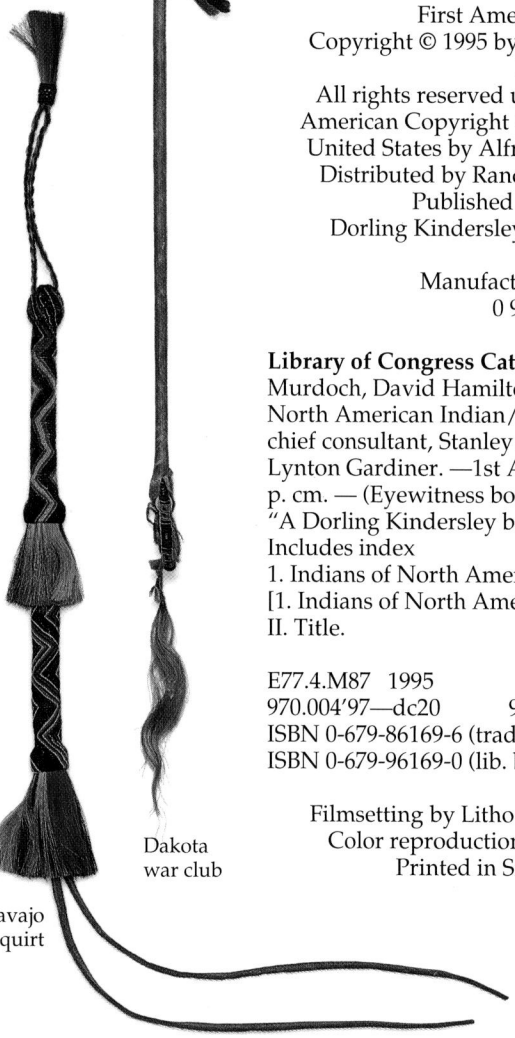

Navajo quirt

Apache war club

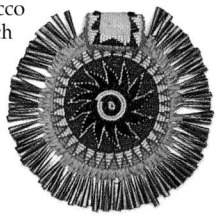

Apache tobacco pouch

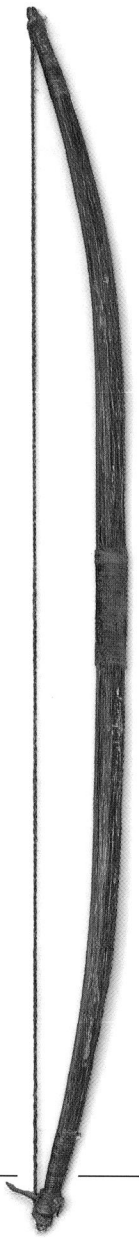

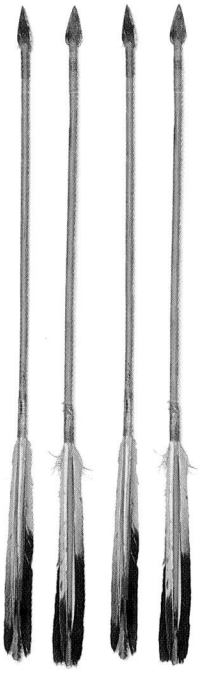

Hopi bow and arrows

A DORLING KINDERSLEY BOOK

Project editor Marion Dent
Art editor Vicky Wharton
Managing editor Simon Adams
Managing art editor Julia Harris
Research Céline Carez
Picture research Sarah Moule
Production Catherine Semark
Editorial consultants Laila Williamson, Department of Anthropology, and Scarlett Lovell, Director of Special Publications, American Museum of Natural History, New York; and Mary Ann Lynch

This is a Borzoi Book published by Alfred A. Knopf, Inc.

This Eyewitness ™ Book has been conceived by Dorling Kindersley Limited and Editions Gallimard

First American edition, 1995

Copyright © 1995 by Dorling Kindersley Limited, London.
All rights reserved under International and Pan-American Copyright Conventions.

Published in the United States by Alfred A. Knopf, Inc., New York. Distributed by Random House, Inc., New York. Published in Great Britain by Dorling Kindersley Limited, London, in 1995.

Manufactured in Singapore
0 9 8 7 6 5 4 3

Library of Congress Cataloging-in-Publication Data
Murdoch, David Hamilton, 1937–
North American Indian/ written by David Murdoch; chief consultant, Stanley A. Freed; photographed by Lynton Gardiner. —1st American ed.
p. cm. — (Eyewitness books)
"A Dorling Kindersley book"—T.p. verso.
Includes index
1. Indians of North America—Juvenile literature.
[1. Indians of North America.] I. Gardiner, Lynton, ill.
II. Title.

E77.4.M87 1995
970.004'97—dc20 94-36193
ISBN 0-679-86169-6 (trade)
ISBN 0-679-96169-0 (lib. bdg.)

Filmsetting by Litho Link Ltd, Welshpool, Powys
Color reproduction by Colourscan, Singapore
Printed in Singapore by Toppan

Contents

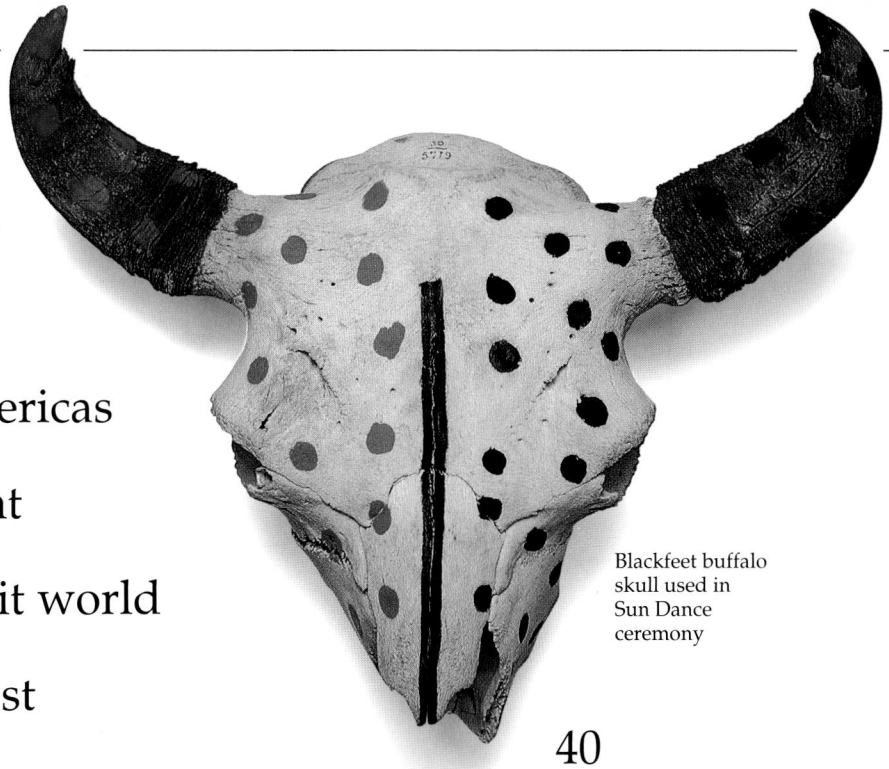

Blackfeet buffalo skull used in Sun Dance ceremony

6
Peopling of the Americas
8
A vast continent
10
Medicine and the spirit world
12
The far Northeast
14
The League of the Iroquois
16
The three sisters
18
The Mid-Atlantic Seaboard
20
The Ohio River Valley
22
Western Great Lakes
24
The settled Southeast
26
The "Five Civilized Tribes"
28
The Great Plains
30
The Dakota (Sioux)
32
Mandan and Hidatsa
34
War and peace
36
The Sun Dance
38
The high Plateau
40
The Great Basin
42
Californian hunter-gatherers
44
The stunning Southwest
46
The Pueblo peoples
48
Apache and Navajo
50
Papago and Pima
52
Land of the totem poles
54
Art second to none
56
The power of potlatch
58
Northern hunters
60
The frozen Arctic
62
Modern times
64
Index

Peopling of the Americas

WHO WERE THE FIRST AMERICANS? Archeologists agree that human beings probably trekked across the Ice Age land bridge from Siberia – but they do not agree on when this happened. Once thought to be 12,000 years ago, the date might be 40,000 years ago according to some new scientific theories. Some present-day Native North Americans believe their sacred stories place their beginnings in America, just as some Christians believe human beings were created in the Garden of Eden. Archeology shows that, however they got here, the first Americans, adapting to changing climate and environment, evolved from hunters using stone-tipped weapons to more advanced societies of farmers and artisans.

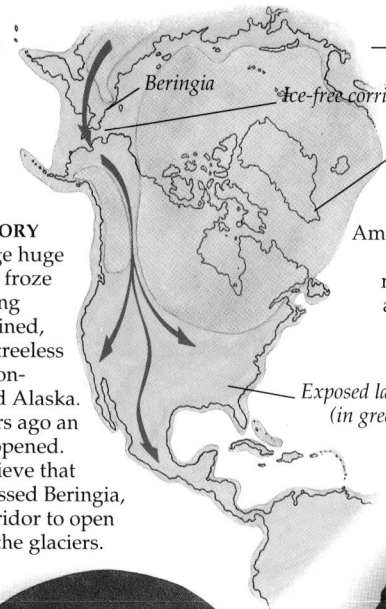

Map of North America showing the human migration route from Siberia across the Ice Age land bridge

MIGRATION THEORY
During the Ice Age huge amounts of water froze into glaciers, Bering Strait became drained, and a wide, low, treeless plain (Beringia) connected Siberia and Alaska. About 12,000 years ago an ice-free corridor opened. Archeologists believe that paleo-Indians crossed Beringia, following the corridor to open country south of the glaciers.

Model of an atlatl – from the Aztec word meaning "spear thrower"

Small Clovis point

Folsom point

Larger Clovis point could measure 5 in (13 cm) in length

Banner stone (a weight of stone) on which spear rested

Wooden bar up to 3 ft (1 m) long

ICE AGE HUNTERS
Definite proof of Ice Age human beings in America came in 1926, with the discovery at Folsom, New Mexico, of carefully shaped stone weapon points dating from 10,000 years ago. In 1932 weapon points from an even older people, up to 12,000 years ago, were unearthed at Clovis, New Mexico.

A STRONGER, LONGER THROW
Hunters of mammoths, mastodons, antique bison, and giant sloths from 10,000 years ago – such as the Folsom people in New Mexico – used an atlatl, a special device for throwing a spear. It was a bar with a flat stone on which the spear rested and a curved tip that engaged the spear's butt. The greater leverage gave a much stronger thrust.

Slate spear point from New England

Copper spear point from the Great Lakes area

Grip of hide with loops for fingers

Chipped-stone spear point from Tennessee

BECOMING EXTINCT
The end of the Ice Age, 10,000 years ago, saw many large animals, like the mammoth, become extinct, perhaps through environmental change or overhunting. From 5000 B.C. to 1000 B.C., the peoples of the Eastern forests learned to hunt woodland game. They lived in permanent settlements and developed complex societies. They were expert toolmakers, making a variety of spear points.

Copper spear point from the Great Lakes region

Polished Anasazi deer-bone spatula

Turquoise and jet inlay

WHY DID THEY DISAPPEAR?
The Anasazi (a Navajo word meaning "ancient enemy") lived on today's Arizona–New Mexico border. By A.D. 1100 they had created the great stone-and-clay buildings later to be called pueblos (pp. 46–47). Their culture faded in the late 1200s, perhaps irreparably damaged by a prolonged drought.

DESERT DWELLERS
The Hohokam people (from the Pima word for "the vanished ones") lived in the desert near the Gila River, Arizona, c. 500 B.C. to A.D. 1500. Expert irrigators, they avoided war, grew corn, built towns, and were superb artisans, making jewelry cleverly cut from shells (left) and fine pottery (below).

Pair of Hohokam shell bracelets

Red-on-buff pottery was traditional Hohokam style

Rare jet ornament found at Pueblo Bonito

Eye made of inlaid turquoise

Frog was symbol of water in Anasazi culture

ANASAZI ARTISANS
Architecture and town design were the noteworthy skills of the Anasazi, their great buildings standing today as reminders of a complex civilization. They also produced interesting pottery and were skilled in working with turquoise (above).

TRADITIONAL STYLE
The Hohokam, predecessors of the Papago and Pima (pp. 50–51), may have been an offshoot of one of the great Central American civilizations, perhaps the Maya. Their early pottery seems similar to ancient Mexican designs. About A.D. 400, they began making striking two-color red-on-buff pots with simple line patterns. Later, more complex designs included animals, human figures, and their gods. The Hohokam cremated their dead, sometimes placing the ashes in these traditional vessels, which were buried.

Mimbres pot, a burial offering, was ritually "killed" by puncturing base to let the spirit escape

Animal head

MOGOLLON–MIMBRES
The Mogollon people (named for their mountain homeland on the Arizona–New Mexico border) lived isolated in mountain valleys c. 300 B.C.– A.D. 1300. The Mimbres, a related group living near New Mexico's Mimbres River, produced remarkable black-on-white pottery from c. A.D. 700. Their artists later created vivid designs of every kind of creature (animal, bird, and human) and geometric patterns – often mixing them.

A vast continent

BY 1500, THE AMERICAN LANDS north of Mexico were home to about 1.3 million people. Over 11,500 years, the descendants of the first Siberian migrants had diverged into more than 300 tribes – the densest population lived east of the Mississippi, in California, and in the Northwest. They had evolved ways of life exploiting food resources in different environments and developed high artistic skills. Their world was constantly changing – game animals became extinct; drought and tribal warfare led to migrations. Over the next 400 years, Europeans would bring about such catastrophic changes as loss of territory, population decline, and cultural restrictions for all Native North Americans.

THE TERROR OF THE PLAINS
In 1500 the Cheyenne were not yet feared Plains warriors (pp. 28–29). Settled in villages in Minnesota, they farmed and hunted. They migrated westward in the mid-1700s, abandoning farming and becoming nomadic Plains horsemen dependent on the buffalo. An eagle-feather war bonnet (left) became their emblem of an experienced and respected warrior.

Ceremonial war bonnet of Cheyenne chief White Eagle

APACHE WARRIOR
The Apache (pp. 48–49) were newcomers in the Southwest in 1500; they seem to have migrated from Canada about 50 years earlier. The Spanish explorer Francisco de Coronado (1510–1554) thought the Chiricahua Apaches he met in 1540 were "a gentle people." Later Spaniards came to disagree with him!

Shaman's headdress of the Tlingit, a Northwest Coast tribe

White eagle feather

Magpie tail feather

Swansdown surrounds painted wooden mask, which represents an eagle

DRIVING OUT EVIL SPIRITS
For the Northwest peoples (pp. 52–57), the spirit world affected every aspect of the tribe's life. Their shamans were revered because they could tap into the spirit world by acquiring a guardian spirit, represented by a fearsome mask with an elaborate headdress. A shaman's powers let him or her predict events, bring good fortune, and cure the sick. Because it was believed that evil spirits caused illness, the shaman fought fire with fire, using the guardian spirit to drive out evil.

TWO TIMUCUA
John White – in the 1580s briefly linked with England's "Lost Colony" at Roanoke in North Carolina – used his artist's skills to portray the tribes he met in the Southeast. Later, he copied pictures of the Florida Timucua (right) made by his friend Jacques le Moyne. White was fascinated by Native peoples and helped create an image in Europe of a gentle and noble people. Sadly, by the 1700s his still-popular pictures fed European bigotry and prejudice; his Native peoples were seen as naked, shameless, heathen savages.

Two Timucua with traditional body tattoos

Roach made of dyed animal hair – an eagle feather was added if a scalp had been taken

Map of North America showing the cultural areas of Native North Americans

ARCTIC
SUBARCTIC
NORTHWEST
PLATEAU
GREAT BASIN
PLAINS
NORTHEAST
CALIFORNIA
SOUTHWEST
SOUTHEAST

DRESSING FOR WAR
In the Western Great Lakes, when village-dwelling Winnebago (pp. 22–23) left to hunt buffalo, they did so on foot. If on a raid, a warrior wore a roach headdress if he had killed but not scalped an enemy. A roach was attached by tying a braid of hair to a flat, thin plate of bone (called a roach spreader), which pressed the headdress to the head.

CULTURAL AREAS
This map shows the ten North American regions whose geography, climate, and resources distinctively shaped the cultures of the tribes who lived in them – eastern farming tribes, settled villages in the Southwest, nomadic buffalo hunters on the Plains, and Inuit in the Arctic. By A.D. 1500 Native peoples spoke over 200 different languages. In a given area two neighbors' speech might be as different as French and German – hence the wide use of sign language on the Plains.

Winnebago roach headdress

Medicine and the spirit world

POWER FILLED THE WORLD of the Native North American. Invisible but everywhere, this supernatural force of the spirit world touched people, animals, and plants. Shamans were special men and women who could heal the sick and capture some of this power to manipulate the ordinary world. Because shamans carried healing herbs, Europeans called them "medicine men," but for a shaman and the tribe all spirit power was "medicine." Shamans used dramatic ceremonies to help a patient's mind reject sickness. They also had drugs. The Five Tribes of the Southeast used the stimulant caffeine and salicylic acid (aspirin). Plains tribes used skunk-cabbage root for asthma and yarrow for minor wounds, both effective remedies. Shamans, like white doctors, were powerless against great European epidemics, especially smallpox which decimated the Native population, falling from 1.3 million people in 1500 to 400,000 before recovering.

George Catlin painting of Old Bear, a Mandan shaman

OLD BEAR
The Mandan, like other Plains tribes, believed visions brought spirit-power. To receive a vision, a Mandan would seek solitude, pray, and abstain from food until near delirium. A truly powerful vision made its recipient a shaman. Dress and equipment (above) would be dictated by the shaman's first and later visions and would therefore contain power.

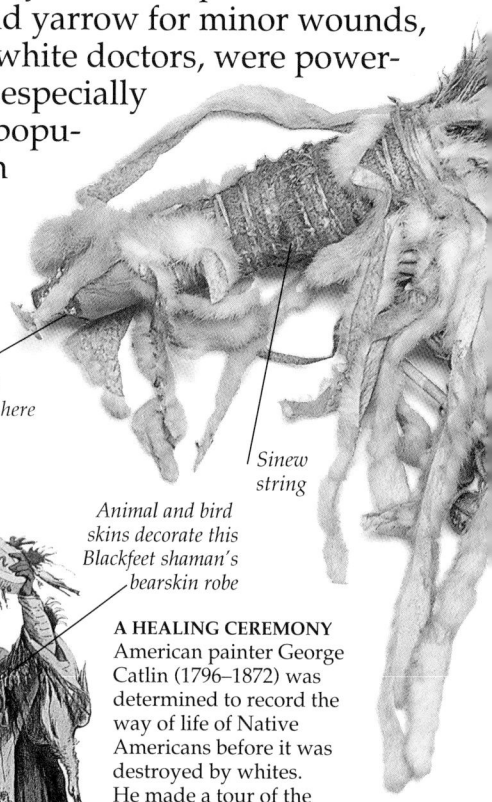

A HEALING CEREMONY
American painter George Catlin (1796–1872) was determined to record the way of life of Native Americans before it was destroyed by whites. He made a tour of the American West (1830–36), having gained the confidence of 48 tribes, and produced over 500 vivid paintings and sketches and detailed notes. This portrait shows a Blackfeet shaman of the Plains performing a healing ceremony. Dressed in a bearskin robe, with the head forming a mask, the shaman danced around the patient.

HOW TO CURE A STOMACHACHE
The Hidatsa Plains tribe dealt with indigestion or other stomach pains by hand massaging or using a stomach pusher (above). With the patient laid flat, the curved end of this instrument (often made of white cedar) was rubbed against the stomach.

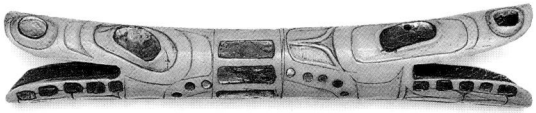

SHAMAN'S SPIRIT HELPER
Like all the tribes of the Northwest, the Quinault believed in a multitude of spirit beings who constantly affected the ordinary world. A shaman's powers came in part from his or her own special guardian spirit. As a doctor casting out an evil spirit, the shaman would carry a carving of the guardian spirit (above).

CATCHING A SOUL
Tsimshian shamans, like those of the other Northwest tribes, believed illness was caused either by an evil spirit or by the loss of the patient's soul – perhaps through a witch's spell. Therefore, one of the shaman's most important instruments was a soul catcher. A carved ivory or bone tube, it captured the soul and returned it to the body. Sometimes blowing through the soul catcher helped to expel the sickness.

FIRST SIGN OF THUNDER
Most revered of the Blackfeet sacred medicine pipes were the thunder pipes. At the first spring thunder, these pipes were removed from their bundles of sacred objects and offered to the thunder spirit. The ceremony asked protection from being struck by lightning (a frequent hazard on the Plains) and also for the power to heal sickness. Possessing a thunder pipe brought great prestige, but it was expected that ownership would be passed on to others.

Blackfeet sacred thunder medicine pipe

Dakota medicine box and herbs

A REMEDY FOR EVERYTHING
In addition to resorting to shamans, with their supernatural powers to cure illness, sick people had available various common medicines obtained from plants. This early 1900s Dakota medicine box contains herbs for headache, earache, stomach pain, bleeding, swelling, and other ailments. The selected herb was reduced to a powder on a tin grater and then steeped in hot water to make a healing tea.

Muslin packet containing herbs, tied with sinew

The far Northeast

Map of North America showing the Northeast Indian lands, including New England, the Mid-Atlantic, Ohio River Valley, and the Western Great Lakes

A LAND OF ABUNDANT CONTRASTS, the wooded Northeast stretched from the St. Lawrence River to present-day North Carolina and west to the Mississippi. Its peoples made the most of an environment rich in game and fish. Except in the very cold far northern areas, they also raised corn, squash, and beans. Northern tribes, like the Penobscot and Malecite, living amid lakes and rivers, developed the birchbark canoe, much envied by their neighbors. From the early 1600s, fur trading with Europeans brought new materials and ideas. However, Northeast peoples (like the powerful Iroquois League) were drawn into the European struggle for North America in the 1700s and were forced to pick sides in the American Revolution (1775–1783) and the War of 1812. Most saw their independence destroyed and some were completely swept away by relentless American settlement.

INGENIOUS DESIGN
Tribes like Nova Scotia's Micmac exploited the fishing resources of their lakes and rivers, using hooks, lines, bows, traps, and spears. They liked to fish at night using birchbark torches. Attracted by the light, the fish came to the surface, where they were speared from birchbark canoes.

KING PHILIP
In 1675, angry and fearful at the growth of European power, "King Philip" (or Metacomet), chief of the Wampanoag, attacked the New England settlements. Eventually the rising was crushed, but if King Philip had formed more effective alliances with other tribes, the English colonies might have been destroyed.

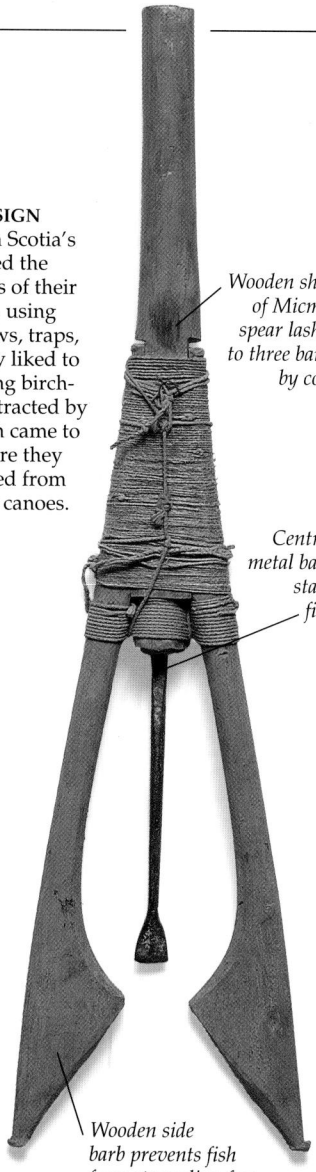

A CROOKED KNIFE
Birch bark was used to make canoes, wigwams, and paper. Bark sheets were cut with knives (like this Penobscot example). Holes were pierced along the edges with an awl and the sheets sewn together with spruce root to make storage or cooking vessels. Two-tone patterns were created by scraping away a dark coating on the bark's inner surface to reveal a lighter color.

Top (right) and side (below) views of model of a Malecite canoe

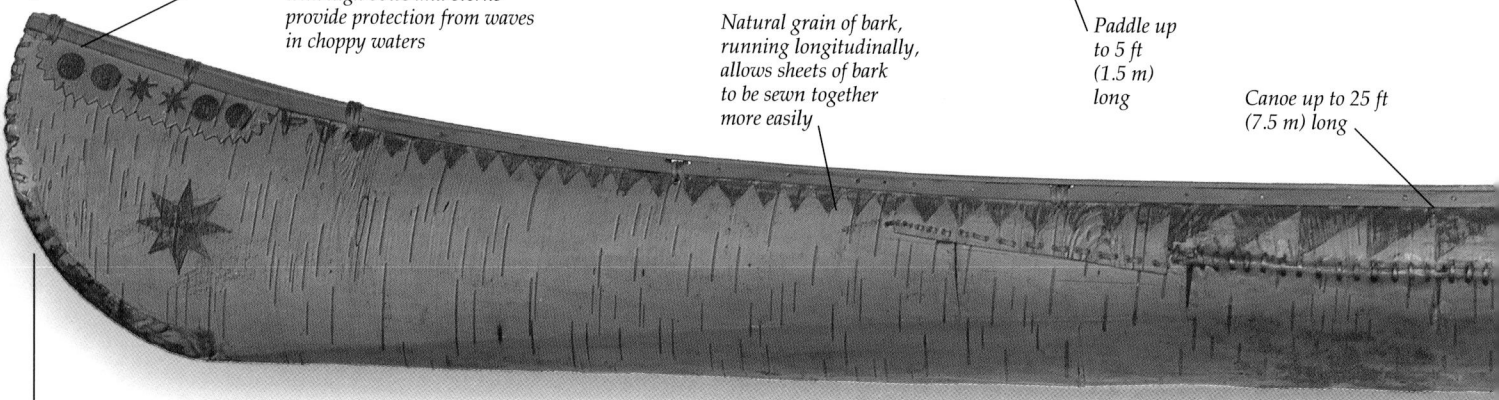

EUROPEAN INFLUENCES
Before contact with Europeans, clothing in the Northeast was usually made from skins, sometimes decorated with painted symbols or dyed porcupine quills. European settlers brought new materials and decorations, such as woven cloth, glass beads, and tailored coats and trousers. The peoples of the Northeast adopted many of these innovations. Northeastern men traditionally wore a skin coat with painted decorations. This Penobscot buckskin jacket shows European influences – a tailored shape and elaborate glass-bead embroidery.

DEER SLAYER
Though the forest peoples were skilled at hunting, success was uncertain. Aid was sought from the spirit world through sacred charms and by rituals to contact the spirits of the slain animals. The chief hunting weapon was the bow and arrow, but a hit might not be fatal. A stone club (like this Penobscot example) was used for killing a wounded deer.

DECORATED DEERSKIN
Like all the peoples of the northeastern forests, the Penobscot wore moccasins of deerskin, which were usually decorated. The influence of the Europeans shows in the lavish use of colored glass beads for decorations and the adoption of flower designs. Floral motifs were copied from white settlers and became widespread in the clothing of the Northeast. Men and women wore the same style of moccasin.

A DESIGN TRIUMPH
The best canoes were made from bark of the white birch, growing only in Canada and the most northeastern U.S. The framework was made of white cedar, split with hammers and wedges. It was covered with large sheets of bark laced together with roots and waterproofed with resin from the black spruce. Light enough to be carried, the canoe could take a load of 4,000 lb (1,800 kg). It was instantly adopted by European explorers and fur traders of the 1600s.

The League of the Iroquois

OUT OF THE NORTHERN WOODS early in the 1600s, there emerged the strongest political and military force in North America. Five tribes – the Mohawk, Onondaga, Seneca, Oneida, and Cayuga – ended their destructive feuding and formed the Iroquois League. Each tribe remained self-governing, but collective decisions were made by a representative Great Council. Though the members were men, they were chosen by the elder women of the tribes, who also had the power to remove them. The League was conceived to bring peace, but it became a formidable war machine. Because it was able to mobilize its forces effectively, it dominated much of the Northeast. Even as late as the mid-1700s it could hold the balance of power in the colonial wars between the French and the British.

CORNPLANTER
Son of a Dutch trader father and a Seneca mother, Cornplanter (1740?–1836) fought Americans during the Revolution (1775–1783). Later this respected Seneca chief became a tireless spokesman for peace, negotiating many treaties.

Stone celt later replaced by steel blade

TRIBES AT WAR
Iroquois wars were usually short raids with weapons like bows and war clubs. Involvement with Europeans competing with each other for the fur trade changed this. In 1649 the Iroquois League, as ally of the Dutch, virtually destroyed the Erie and Huron tribes, who supported the French.

Rattle made from a whole turtle shell

MOHAWK MUSIC
Music for the Mohawk, as for other eastern peoples, mostly depended on drums and rattles. A turtle-shell rattle was made by drying the animal, then cleaning out the shell, being careful to leave the head, tail, and legs intact. After this, pebbles were inserted and a wooden handle added.

HIAWATHA – A HERO
In the late 1500s, the prophet Dekanawidah, despairing at constant intertribal warfare, saw Iroquois union in a vision. Hiawatha, a Mohawk, then traveled ceaselessly between the tribes, persuading them to unite. *Hiawatha*, the famous poem by Henry Longfellow (1807–1882), gives no indication of the charisma and diplomatic skills of this remarkable leader.

Iroquois belts woven from wampum could be many feet long

Purple beads were twice as costly as white ones

THE COLOR PURPLE
Strings of purple and white tubular shell beads, called wampum, were used as symbolic gifts at marriages, as condolence to the bereaved, or as an invitation to ceremonies such as peace negotiations or a war alliance. White was the color of peace, black of gloomy matters. Purple was the most prized. Realizing the high value placed on it by the tribes, Europeans manufactured wampum from shell, using it in trade as money. Then they began to counterfeit it in glass. As money, wampum became debased and fell out of use.

Iroquois war club made in typical "rabbit's hind-leg" style

Elm-bark covering

Model of a four-fire, eight-family longhouse

MAGNIFICENT MASKS, MYSTERIOUS MEDICINE

The False Face Society was a group of healers who used the powers they derived from the spirit world to cure ailments mostly involving the head, shoulders, or limbs. Headache cures were popular. Ceremonies, held at the patient's invitation in the longhouse, were short because of the great power of the False Faces. A cured patient was obligated to become a member of the Society, to help others. Every spring and fall the False Faces would visit each Iroquois household to purify it spiritually and exorcise disease.

LONGHOUSE STYLE

The Iroquois lived in long-houses up to 25 ft (7.5 m) wide and 150 ft (45 m) long. They had a frame of wooden poles covered with elm bark. Compartments with low sleeping platforms for up to 12 families lined the sides. Shared cooking fires were spaced along a central aisle.

Storage pits for corn were dug into the ground at key points within the village.

The three sisters

CORN WAS LIFE for tribes throughout the eastern woodlands. Producing starch to make energy, corn can provide 75 percent of the human body's food needs. Many corn varieties were grown (the Iroquois raised 15), and none required much labor. No care was necessary after planting the seed, except for scaring off birds, until the harvest. Beans and squash were often planted in the same field. Beans twined up the cornstalks, and squash choked weeds and kept the ground moist. The Iroquois believed these crops had spirit beings and called them "the three sisters." Dried and stored, corn, beans, and squash guaranteed food supplies, and more time could be devoted to ceremonies, hunting, trading, and war.

AUTUMN TREAT
Ripening in the autumn, pumpkin squash is a valuable vegetable. English colonists learned its use from Native Americans and invented sweet pumpkin pie, traditional at Thanksgiving.

Iroquois wooden bowl containing dried beans

BOWL OF BEANS
Depending on environment and accidents of history, many varieties of bean were grown across the continent. All had the same important qualities. They were a good extra food source because they had high amounts of proteins and essential vitamins (particularly of the Vitamin B group). Equally important, beans can be dried and stored for long periods, even years, without spoiling.

Ojibwa bark basket with dried rings of Sauk and Fox (Western Great Lakes tribes) squash plaited together

Seneca wooden pestle

Mohawk mortar made from hollowed-out tree trunk

DRIED SQUASH
Squashes grew thoughout the summer, when they were eaten fresh, providing an important source of Vitamin C, essential for general health. A portion of the crop was cut into strips or rings and sun-dried, or hung up whole inside the dwelling until dry, then stored with the beans and corn.

GRINDING CORN
Iroquois women shucked (stripped) the corncob of kernels with deer jawbones, then boiled the kernels in lye (made from boiled ashes) to soften the skins. Next the lye and skins were washed away in a special basket and the kernels were dried. They were turned into meal by laborious pounding with a mortar and pestle (left).

Iroquois harvesting basket containing cobs of Oneida dried corn

CORN ON THE COB
Some corn had to be saved for the lean winter months. Cobs were dried and hung in the longhouse. Some cobs were shucked and the kernels dried and stored in bins or underground granaries. Ground corn kernels were boiled as a porridge or made into cakes and eaten with maple sugar, honey, or fat.

MIDWINTER CEREMONIAL

The most solemn of the Iroquois ceremonies was held at midwinter, around the first of February. Messengers would stir the ashes of each longhouse fire, symbolizing the start of a new year. At the end of the four-day ceremony, the secret societies performed ritual dances. Among these was the Husk Face Society, whose members believed they were linked to spirit beings particularly connected with farming. Wearing sacred masks made from braided and sewn cornhusks, they danced to persuade the spirit world to ensure a good harvest and the birth of many children.

Holes left for eyes and mouth

Loose ends of cornhusks represent hair

Iroquois Husk Face made of individual cornhusk braids sewn together to form a face

Cherokee (of Tennessee) basket for sifting cornmeal

FINE TUNING

The contribution of Cherokee men to crop raising was clearing the land. Trees were felled by cutting a circle in the bark (the dead trunk was later burned). Women then hoed the soil and made small mounds in which to plant the corn. Usually, two crops were sown, a summer crop to be eaten and a fall crop to be dried and stored for winter. After husking and washing, the corn was ground into meal. The meal was then shaken through a sifter basket, like a modern sieve, to remove the coarse fragments.

MAKING A MEAL OF IT

After husking, drying, and shucking (stripping kernels off the cob), Iroquois women had a long, hard job making corn into meal. Dried kernels were pounded in a wooden mortar and pestle (far left), or cracked and ground between two stones. A wooden bowl served to catch the meal.

SPRING PLANTING

In 1564, the French explorer Le Moyne made drawings of the Timucua in Florida. In his picture of them planting spring corn, they look more like French peasants than Native Americans. The Timucua men used hoes with fish-bone heads (not iron-headed mattocks) and the women planted seeds in holes, not loosely scattering them.

The Mid-Atlantic Seaboard

A LAND OF WOODED PLAINS and lush valleys extended along the Mid-Atlantic Seaboard (Delaware, Maryland, Virginia, and North Carolina). Its people lived in villages of bark-covered, domed or arch-roofed dwellings. They raised corn and hunted in the forests. They were led by sachems (chiefs), who ruled by consensus. In 1585 John White, briefly part of the English colony at Roanoke (North Carolina) before it mysteriously disappeared, made paintings of the Secotan. Later published as engravings, they became the European stereotype of "Indians" for the next 200 years. When the English settled the colony of Virginia, they encountered the strong Powhatan alliance, which nearly destroyed them. Even more powerful were the Delaware, a confederation whose influence in the 1600s stretched far to the north and west. Their power was later broken by the Iroquois.

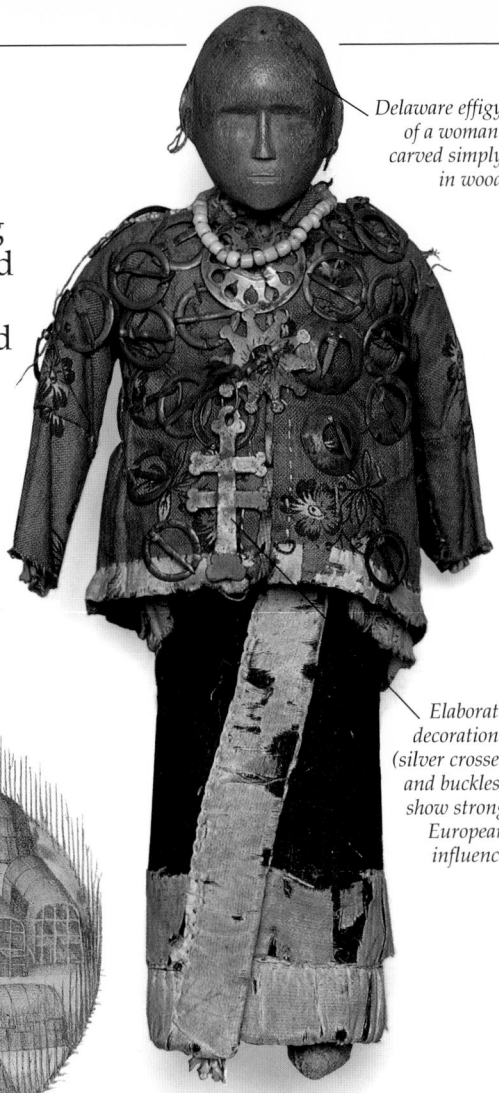

A SECOTAN VILLAGE
John White (pp. 8–9) painted this scene of a typical Secotan village in 1585. Shown are houses of bent saplings covered with bark and woven mats, surrounded by a defensive palisade (a circle of upright posts). The houses with sleeping platforms resemble those of the Iroquois to the north. The building with the cupola is a temple. Eventually the Secotan disappeared from their territory in North Carolina and were succeeded by other tribes.

A DOLL FOR HEALTH
The Delaware believed in the universal presence of the Great Spirit, and also in a world filled with lesser spirit beings. Spirits shaped their lives, fortunes, and health. Prayers, offerings, and ceremonies were meant to seek the help of these beings. This wooden image is a woman spirit guardian of health. Every fall the Delaware honored her with a feast, presents, and the sacrifice of a deer.

WOODLAND ART
With abundant forests, Eastern tribes used wood for many household utensils, such as bowls, spoons, and ladles. Woodworking was a task for men. To make hollow vessels like this bowl, the wood was first charred and the burned part scraped away with a stone (later iron) knife. Carved from the burled (knotty) parts of elm and maple, these objects were both useful and an expression of woodland art.

Simply carved wooden Delaware serving bowl and spoon

Handy hook topped with a crown

Handle ornately carved with turtle, horse, and horseshoe

Paddle intricately carved with a star

Delaware wooden food stirrer

Bottom filled with stones to sink basket to river bed

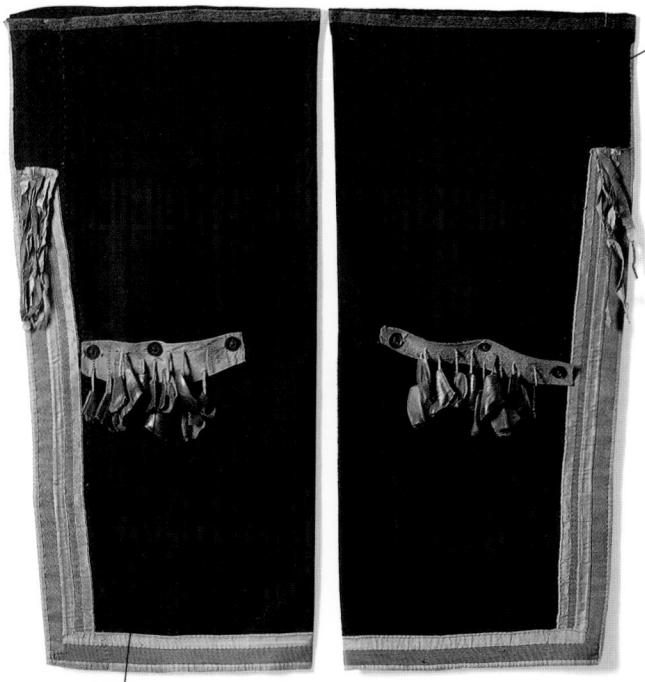

Delaware leggings made of woven cloth

Decorated with deer-hoof rattles and silk ribbon appliqué

WEARING APPAREL
Most clothing was made from animal skins, particularly deer hide. Men, taught from boyhood to ignore rain and chilly weather, wore only a breechcloth (front and back flaps held up by a belt) and moccasins in the warmer months, together with buckskin leggings. Women wore a waist-to-knee skirt over knee-high leggings. In winter both men and women added a fur robe. European contact brought woven cloth (left), which was sometimes substituted for skins, and new clothing patterns, such as jackets and trousers.

POCAHONTAS'S WEDDING
In 1607 Captain John Smith (1580–1631), from the English colony of Virginia, was captured by the chief of the Powhatan. Smith's life was dramatically saved by the pleadings of the chief's daughter, Pocahontas (1595–1617). Kidnapped by the English, she met and later married John Rolfe (1585–1622). This marriage kept the peace between the English and the Powhatans until the chief's death in 1618.

TRAPPING FISH
Fish were an important addition to forest game all over the Eastern woodlands, not least because they could be caught all year round. Fish were speared, shot with bows, or taken with hook and line. Where some species migrated upriver to spawn, they could be caught by using nets, weirs, or traps (below).

Large handle for carrying awkwardly shaped trap

Loosely woven splint construction

Fish swam into opening but could not turn around once inside

Powhatan fish trap

TRADITIONAL DRESS
Crowded out of their 17th-century homeland in Pennsylvania and New Jersey by colonial settlement, most Delaware had finally settled in Indian Territory (Oklahoma) by 1830. Traditional dress persisted among women, as seen in this photograph of a mother and daughter from the early 1900s. Nellie Longhat (far right) and her mother are wearing cotton dresses with capes decorated with silver brooches, bead-embroidered moccasins, and an accumulation of bead necklaces.

The Ohio River Valley

THE FERTILE LANDS OF THE GREAT VALLEY drained by the Ohio River and its many tributaries (from Illinois east to Pennsylvania and south to Tennessee) offered a rich environment for two great prehistoric cultures, the Adena and later the Hopewell, which together spanned about 1500 years to A.D. 500. The Hopewell culture spread from the Eastern Great Lakes to the Gulf of Mexico and west of the Mississippi. The Hopewell created large burial mounds – almost all we know about them comes from excavating these earthworks. Spectacular artists and artisans, they imported exotic raw materials from a vast trade network. The Hopewell faded as quickly as they had arisen, and simpler hunter-farmer tribes slowly took their place. In the 1700s, France and Britain, with their tribal allies, fought for control of the Ohio Valley as the key to dominating North America. From the 1790s, relentless white American settlement created a short-lived intertribal resistance movement led by the Shawnee statesman Tecumseh.

GRAVE IMAGES
The Hopewell people buried their dead surrounded by their wealth: ornaments, jewelry, fine stone tools, and pottery. Some of these may have been specially made as grave objects, like these small clay figurines (above). The burial sites give us our only knowledge of the Hopewell people's appearance, clothing, and ornaments, though probably only of those rich enough to afford large burial mounds.

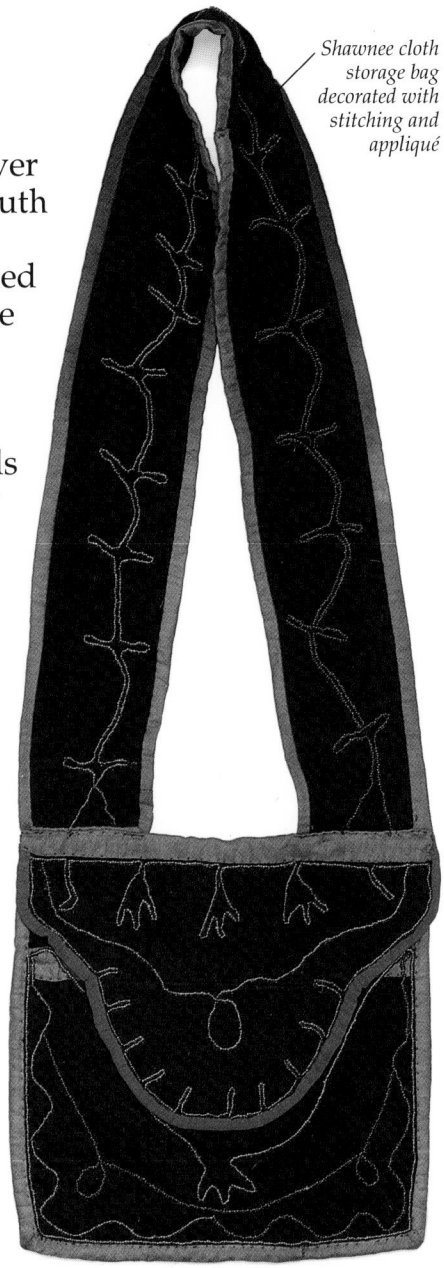

IN THE BAG
The Shawnee were a powerful force in the Ohio Valley in the late 1700s. They tried to become a barrier to American westward expansion, but they were defeated by General "Mad Anthony" Wayne in 1794. In 1831 they sold what was left of their lands and moved to Oklahoma.

STRIKING BIRD
Hopewell stone-carving shows the same artistry as their other work. Most striking are stone pipes carved in the shape of animals or birds, such as this raven (above). Most, called platform pipes, had a base on which rested the carved figure containing the bowl for tobacco. The smoker drew the smoke through a hole bored through the base.

MIAMI ALLIANCES
Along with their Ohio Valley allies, the Miami suffered defeats in the 1790s and in the War of 1812. However, trade with whites continued and brought items such as wool, silk ribbon, metal brooches, and glass beads. Miami women used them to add prestige to their clothing and developed techniques to get striking effects, such as the skillful appliqué and nickel-silver decoration on this woolen skirt from the early 1800s.

A POTAWATOMI POUCH
For Native Americans, the great issue of the late 1700s was maintaining the Ohio River as the boundary between white settlers and themselves. Like the Miami and Shawnee, the Potawatomi fought to stop the settlers. After several defeats, they and other tribes signed peace treaties in 1815. Despite hostilities, they traded with whites for new clothing materials, so that only bags, tobacco pouches (above), and moccasins continued to be regularly made from deerskin.

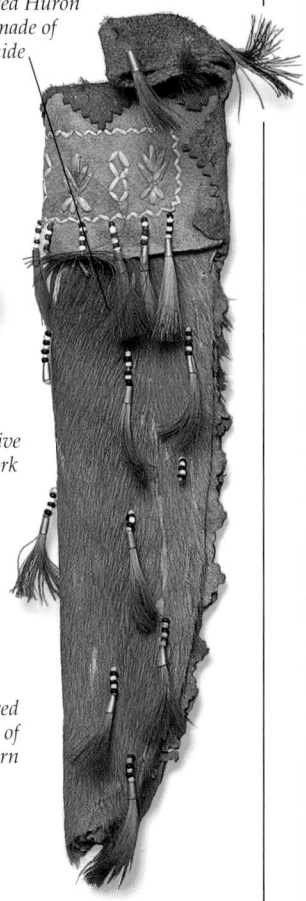

HURON HUNTERS
The Huron were long-standing enemies of the Iroquois, who dealt them a stunning defeat in 1649. James Fenimore Cooper (1789–1851), who wrote *The Last of the Mohicans*, made the Iroquois the villains of some of his stories. This Huron skinning-knife sheath is decorated with beads, appliqué stitching, and animal hair.

THE GREAT TECUMSEH
Tecumseh (1768–1813) used his great political skills to forge a tribal alliance opposing white advance into the Midwest. With his shaman twin brother Tenskwatawa (1768–1836), he argued that land could be ceded only with the consent of all the tribes. Despite his belief in peaceful negotiation, in 1811 white forces destroyed the league at the Battle of Tippecanoe (Indiana). Embittered, Tecumseh joined the British (who made him a general) against the U.S. in the War of 1812, in which he was killed.

Western Great Lakes

THE PEOPLES OF THE WESTERN GREAT LAKES (west of Michigan) took full advantage of their access to both woodlands and prairies. In summer the women of tribes such as the Sauk and Fox planted corn and squash while the men hunted buffalo. The Menominee harvested huge quantities of wild rice – their name comes from the Ojibwa name for this plant. In winter the tribes turned to semi-nomadic hunting, living in portable lodges of poles and reed mats as they followed game. The tribes traded with each other, but also were regularly at war. From the early 1600s a powerful force was the Midewiwin, a shaman secret society devoted to healing and encouraging correct behavior as a guarantee of good health.

Male doll given the husband's name, female doll the wife's name

Love medicine is placed in breast of each Menominee doll

Grizzly bear claws separated by triplets of blue beads

MEDICINE DOLLS
Shamans used human figures as "medicine" to control others' behavior. The Menominee used "love dolls" (above) tied face-to-face to ensure that a husband and wife would be faithful to each other. The Potawatomi used dolls as charms to make one person fall in love with another.

SWEET AS MAPLE SUGAR
Maple sugar was greatly valued, used not only on fruit and corn cakes but also as a seasoning on meat and fish. Collection began in late March. Each tree was gashed and a cedarwood spout inserted to allow the sap to drain into a birchbark bucket. Whole Menominee communities moved into the woods, where each family had its own group of trees and a special wigwam.

Ojibwa sap skimmer

Ojibwa wooden trough and Menominee ladle (far left)

MAKING MAPLE SUGAR
First the sap was boiled to reduce its water content. Boiling was done by dropping heated rocks into birchbark containers. After boiling and skimming, the resulting syrup was strained through fiber matting and poured into a wooden trough. As it cooled, it was worked back and forth with a ladle until it formed granules.

SUGAR CONES
Sugar was stored in birchbark containers for use during the year. Some might be forced into molds, such as these Ojibwa cones (right), much like those Europeans used for making conical sugar loaves from cane sugar.

BEAR-CLAW NECKLACE
Necklaces of grizzly bear claws were greatly prized, not least because of the difficulty of persuading their original fearsome owners to part with the main components! Usually the property of a chief or renowned warrior, bear claws were often passed from one generation to another.

CHIEF KEOKUK
Unlike his rival Black Hawk (1767–1838) who fought a hopeless war against settlers in 1832, uk chief Keokuk (1780?–1848) realized that his eople had to leave Illinois. His tribe honored him for establishing their claim, and that of the politically affiliated Fox, to territory in present-day Iowa. His realism is shown in his avoiding the fate of Black Hawk's followers, destroyed in their war with the U.S. government.

THE SUPERNATURAL
A person who could gain extraordinary power from the spirit world became a shaman. A spirit being, appearing in visions, taught the shaman the uses of many substances (bones, roots, skins), which were stored in a medicine bag (above). Shamans used their power to cure illnesses and to bring success in war and hunting.

Bear-claw necklace of the Fox tribe

WAR OR PEACE PIPE?
Tobacco was thought to have special powers. It was used in offerings to please spirit beings. The Menominee also believed smoking increased their wisdom. At important ceremonies, tribes smoked the sacred calumet, which was passed around clockwise. Because this often marked the end of fighting, the calumet is usually called a peace pipe, but it was also used in the war council.

The settled Southeast

RICH IN FLORA AND FAUNA, with fertile soils and a mild climate, the Southeast was an ideal environment. As skilled builders, artisans, and farmers, with a wide knowledge of medicine, the Southeastern peoples created a flourishing civilization. From A.D. 800 to 1500, the Southeast's Temple Mound Builders developed large towns, traded widely, and held great ceremonies. The rulers lived luxuriously while commoners toiled. The flat-topped mounds seen in the region today are the community sites of this vanished people. The historic Natchez tribe, which also built mounds topped by temples, may have survived the Mound Builders. Contacted by the Europeans in the late 1600s, the Natchez came under pressure from colonists to cede land but fought back. Three wars with the French in the 1700s destroyed their nation, scattering the survivors throughout the Southeast.

Map of North America showing the Southeast region

THE ANNUAL BUSK
The Green Corn Ceremony (Busk) was the most important rite of the Southeast. It was held when the corn ripened, offering thanks for the harvest and marking the beginning of a new year. It involved ritual purification, dancing around a sacred fire, and a celebratory feast.

Yuchi (of Tennessee) feather fan carried by dancers

Color of fan echoed color of Busk – spectators and dancers alike were dressed in white

Thatched roof

Pole frame

Sleeping platform

Mud wall

Model of a Natchez house

SUNS AND STINKARDS
Successor to the Temple Mound Builders, the Natchez (of Louisiana) amazed French explorers with their complex hierarchical society and elaborate ceremonies. Ruled by an all-powerful monarch, the Great Sun, Natchez society was divided into Suns, nobles, honored men, and commoners (stinkards). The main village had houses such as the one above, and on a mound, a temple that sheltered an eternal flame.

Wooden lacrosse stick measured up to 3 ft (1 m) long

A TWO-HANDLED, THREE-LEGGED POT
Women made the pottery in the Southeast. The clay was cleaned and mixed, and long clay cylinders were layered on top of a small clay disk. A wetted shell was used to smooth the clay, thin the walls, and shape the pot. Before firing, the pot was polished with a smooth pebble and designs cut in with a pointed wooden tool.

Finely etched decoration

Catawba (of South Carolina) pot based on ancient techniques

SHELL GORGET
The Temple Mound people often used decoratively incised shells as ornaments. This gorget (a plate hung around the neck to rest on the chest) has the image of a long-nosed god. Unfortunately, because these people had no writing, our knowledge of their beliefs is fragmentary.

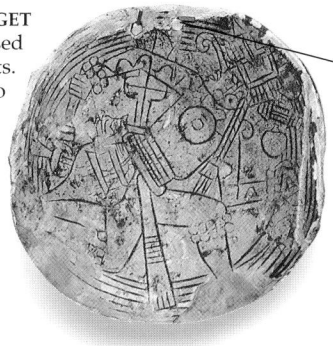

Hole for string to allow gorget to be hung from neck

Skin-covered Yuchi lacrosse ball stitched together with sinew

Perfectly rounded chunkey disk made of highly polished stone

A CHUNKEY STONE
A popular Temple Mound Builders sport was "chunkey." One player rolled a polished stone disk down a court 100 ft (30 m) long. Then he and his opponent threw wooden lances to mark where they guessed the disk would fall over. The game was still played in the Southeast when the Europeans arrived.

Loosely woven webbing made of thin strips of hide

Heavily woven webbing showing more intricate style

Each stick is made of a single piece of bent wood

Thin strips of hide lash the two ends together

Yuchi lacrosse stick

HOW TO PLAY LACROSSE
Known to many Native North American peoples, the stick-and-ball game that French explorers called lacrosse was played with fanatical enthusiasm in the Southeast. Teams had 100 players each, often many more. Each player used two sticks with webbed ends to catch and throw a ball made of wood or stuffed deerskin, ultimately aiming to hurl it between the opposing team's goalposts.

Special designs painted on face and body

Mane worn around neck

Each player is allowed to hold two lacrosse sticks

Beaded belt

Long, rigid horsetail

DRAMATIC PAINTINGS
American artist George Catlin (1796–1872) painted several dramatic pictures of lacrosse in 1834. This portrait shows Thirsts-for-Stone, an outstanding Choctaw (of Mississippi) lacrosse player, wearing his best game outfit (right). He would have drunk sacred medicine and performed ritual dances before the game. The women of the village, accompanied by medicine men, sought aid from the spirit world for their team through dances and song.

George Catlin painting of a Choctaw ball game

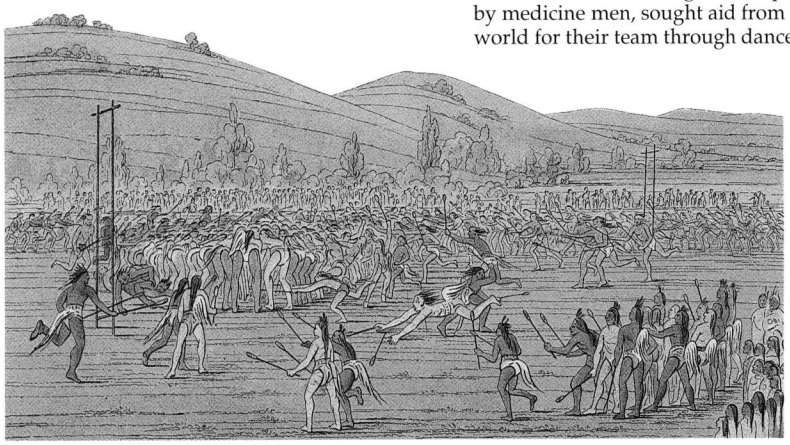

LITTLE BROTHER OF WAR
Lacrosse as played in the Southeast was so violent that the Indians called it the "little brother of war." Serious injuries were commonplace and players sometimes were killed. Challenge matches between villages or tribes drew perhaps a thousand rival supporters. Spectators bet heavily on the result.

The "Five Civilized Tribes"

A REMARKABLE CIVILIZATION had grown up in the lush Southeast by the late 1500s. The tribes lived in planned villages, were skilled farmers as well as hunters, and had advanced medical knowledge. Three hundred years later they had adopted American agricultural methods and had put their laws in written form. Many had become Christians. All this made no difference to the whites, who were determined to seize their tribal lands. In the 1830s, the Choctaw, followed by the Cherokee, Chickasaw, Creek, and finally Seminole (called the "Five Civilized Tribes" by the whites), were forcibly moved to Oklahoma. Many died on the trail.

DRESSING UP
Seminole dolls show how women, up to the early 1900s, combed their hair around a frame and wore skirts and capes of strips of cotton cloth in contrasting colors. A girl was given a string of beads when young and added strings throughout her life, until they almost reached her ears – and weighed several pounds.

Fine beadwork fit for a chief

THE EAGLE DANCE
Before contact with Europeans, a most important Cherokee ceremony was the Eagle Dance, held as part of the rites celebrating both peace and war. Dancers wore eagle feathers on their heads and waved eagle-feather wands to the music of drums and rattles.

Smaller feathers attached with sinew to both ends of wooden handle

Feathers decorate Cherokee Eagle Dance wand

CHIEF OF THE CHOCTAW
The Choctaws' home was in Mississippi and Louisiana, until most were removed by the U.S. government to a reservation in Indian Territory, which was later called Oklahoma (the Choctaw name for "red people"). A chief of those Choctaw who managed to stay in Louisiana wore this sash at his wedding in 1871.

Small entrance leading into windowless house

Wall made of dried mud smoothed onto gatelike framework of small poles

A LITTLE HUT BY THE WATER
In hot, humid Florida, such as the Everglades swamps, the Seminole lived in open-sided dwellings (chickees). Made from palmetto poles with thatched roofs, these huts were built on platforms to avoid flooding from the heavy rains.

MAKING MUSIC
Southeastern ceremonies and games were accompanied by music made by drums and rattles. A water drum had a deerskin stretched over a hollow log containing water so that it resonated. Rattles were made from dried turtle shells, cattle horns, or gourds.

Creek rattle made of hollowed-out gourd filled with corn kernels or small stones to make sounds

THE UNDEFEATED SEMINOLE
Originally mostly Creek from Georgia and Alabama, the Seminole (left) fled to Florida (their name means "runaway") in the 1700s, where they were joined by many runaway slaves. The Seminole fought two wars with the U.S. The second (1835–42) began with the government's efforts to remove them to Oklahoma. Led by the great Osceola (below), the Seminole fought U.S. forces to a standstill. Although many Seminole surrendered in 1841–42 and were sent west, others remained in Florida's Everglades swamps, undefeated. A treaty was signed with them only in 1934, ending possibly the longest war in history.

Conical roof made up of several poles running from the circumference at the bottom of the structure

A MEETING HOUSE
Creek village dwellings were carefully organized into cool summer houses and warm winter lodges. In summer the Council of Elders met in a square surrounded by sun shelters, and in a round house up to 25 ft (7.5 m) high in bad weather. This council house was also used for ceremonies and festivities.

George Catlin painting of Osceola

SEMINOLE HERO
In 1835, enraged by an agreement to move the Seminole to Oklahoma, Osceola (1804–38) killed a rival chief to become leader of those who were determined to stay in their Florida homeland. Small bands of guerrilla forces were led by Osceola against 10,000 U.S. troops until he was captured through a dishonorable false truce.

Roof made of thin tree trunks, covered with bark sheeting to provide extra protection from heavy rains

Central fire

Model of Creek council house in which elders are holding a meeting

The Great Plains

A SEA OF GRASS stretched more than 2,000 miles (3,200 km) north to south between the Rocky Mountains and the Mississippi River. In 1800 this area supported about 150,000 people and 60 million buffalo, all sharing 1 million sq miles (2.5 million sq km) of territory. With sparse rainfall on the western Plains, tribes there were dependent on the huge herds of buffalo, unlike tribes of the better-watered eastern prairie, who combined farming with buffalo hunting. Buffalo migrations dictated the way of living for the 30 Plains tribes. The buffalo meant not just a crucial source of meat – their hides, hair, and horns made dwellings, clothing, tools, and utensils. Before the Spanish brought horses to the Southwest in the 1500s, nomadic Plains tribes traveled and hunted on foot. Of all Native North Americans, Plains peoples were the finest horsemen. Their riding skills dominated the style of their incessant warfare.

Wooden bow reinforced with sinew glued to the back

Plains warrior carried about 20 arrows in his quiver

Map of North America showing the Plains region

Bowstring made of twisted buffalo sinew

DISTANCE WEAPON
Until the Plains tribes acquired guns from the Europeans, bows and arrows were their only effective long-distance weapon. Made from warp-resistant hardwoods, reinforced with sinew strips, and firing arrows tipped with stone (replaced by iron points after Europeans introduced this metal), the bows were only about 3 ft (1 m) in length for easy use on horseback.

Strap for slinging bow case and quiver across rider's back

HUNTING ON HORSEBACK
Before horses, Plains hunters killed buffalo by stampeding hundreds at a time over a cliff. A lone hunter disguised as a wolf might creep up on a buffalo until he was within bowshot. Later, mounted hunters approached stealthily until the herd ran, then raced alongside the fleeing animals to fire at point-blank range – as dramatically shown in this detail from a George Catlin painting.

Long travois poles were also used to make a tepee

HORSE TRAVOIS
Nomadic tribes transported their belongings by using horse-drawn or dog-drawn travois – an A-frame of spruce poles lashed with rawhide and fixed to a saddle. A horse could drag a 300-lb (135-kg) load up to 12 miles (20 km) per day.

Dakota hide quiver and bow case decorated with glass beads; before beads were available, flattened, dyed porcupine quills were used

Two Blackfeet women and child with horse travois

PLAINS BALL GAME
The Plains peoples played games that tested qualities important to their way of life, such as speed and strength. The most popular game among women was shinny. Two teams armed with curved or straight sticks struggled to get the ball (below) past each other's goalposts. The ball could be batted or kicked but not touched with the hand. Men also played, and sometimes a men's team might challenge a women's.

HAVE TEPEE WILL TRAVEL
For the nomadic hunting tribes, the tepee was a highly practical dwelling, cool in summer and warm in winter. Constructed from a cone of long poles covered with buffalo hides sewn together, it could be erected by two women in an hour. About 15 ft (5 m) in diameter, it comfortably housed a family, their bedding, and their belongings. Tepees were usually decorated with traditional painted designs.

Two sticks used in a Plains Cree throwing game

Model of Arapaho Grass Dancer

GRASS DANCE
In the late 1800s a new ceremony, the Grass Dance, spread throughout the Plains tribes. Originally an Omaha ritual that recalled men's courage and achievements in war, it became a social dance with songs and costumes. To a people threatened with the destruction of their way of life, the Grass Dance became, and remains, a symbol of Native North American solidarity.

The Dakota (Sioux)

THE LORDS OF THE NORTHERN PLAINS by the mid-1800s were the Dakota, called Sioux by Europeans (from an Ojibwa word for "enemy"). In the 1700s they had been forced westward by well-armed Ojibwa from their Western Great Lakes homeland. The Dakota were made up of seven independent groups, ranging from Minnesota west to the Upper Missouri River. The largest of the Plains tribes and outstanding warriors, the Dakota terrorized their Indian enemies and offered fierce resistance to whites. Their lives depended on the buffalo – and the end of the great herds meant the end of their independence. Between 1862 and 1877 they forcefully resisted the U.S. advance into their lands. In 1876, in eastern Montana near the Little Bighorn River, they inflicted on the U.S. Army the most famous defeat by Native North Americans.

USING A BOW AND ARROW
Dakota children were taught proper behavior and encouraged to imitate adults. They were treated with much affection and rarely punished. They were expected, however, to learn skills at a young age. Boys practiced shooting with half-sized bows and arrows (above), first at targets, then at small game, and began hunting seriously in their early teens. Girls were expected to help their mothers in strenuous outside work.

Geometric beadwork style was favored by the Dakota

Unadorned fringed central flap

Flank strap (cinch) of heavy cotton

Hide strap for tying items to saddle

Buffalo rawhide covers wooden stirrup

BETTER THAN BAREBACK
Though Plains tribes long rode bareback, a saddle and stirrups gave better stability and control. The Dakota "pad saddle" was made from two pieces of tanned hide stitched together and stuffed with buffalo or deer hair. It had hardly any cantle to support the rider's back, or pommel at the front. Stirrups, usually wooden, were attached by a rawhide strap.

Detail from 1881 pictograph of the Battle of the Little Bighorn, painted on a buffalo hide (below)

THE BATTLE OF THE LITTLE BIGHORN
Gold seekers invading the sacred Black Hills in South Dakota, guaranteed to the Dakota by treaty, brought about war in 1876. A U.S. Army unit moved against a huge force of Dakota and Cheyenne, not realizing their numbers. General George A. Custer (1839–76) impetuously attacked with an advance guard. On June 25, 1876, he and his 215 men were all killed.

DEATH ON THE PLAINS
The Dakota did not bury their dead. Instead, the body was wrapped in a buffalo robe and placed beyond the reach of wild animals on a platform supported by poles. Warriors had their weapons and medicine pouch hung beside them, women their important household utensils. Relatives mourned beside the body.

THE ART OF QUILLWORK
Before white traders arrived with beads, Plains women took great pride in their quilling skills. Women's saddlebags were made in pairs to hang on each side of a saddle or to store household articles in a tepee.

OLD MAN OF THE PLAINS
Ceremonial dress for a Dakota elder in the mid-1800s marked his status. His headdress of eagle tail feathers (thought to have spirit power) could be worn only by a proven warrior. His costume was completed by bear paws, beaded leggings, and quilled moccasins. A headdress such as this was presented to Sitting Bull when he became a chief of the Teton Dakota.

SITTING BULL
A medicine man who was chosen principal chief of the Teton Dakota in 1868, Sitting Bull (1834?–90) displayed great qualities of leadership. In 1876, with Chief Crazy Horse (1849?–77), he united the Dakota to fight the U.S. army and succeeded in destroying Custer's unit. Later pardoned, he starred in the Wild West Show of Buffalo Bill (William Cody, 1846–1917).

CRADLE WILL ROCK
A Dakota baby spent much of its time in a cradleboard. A lace-up skin bag on a wooden framework, it could be strapped to a mother's back, hung from a saddle, tied to a travois, or just propped upright. A decorated cradleboard like this would usually be made by the sister of the baby's father.

Mandan and Hidatsa

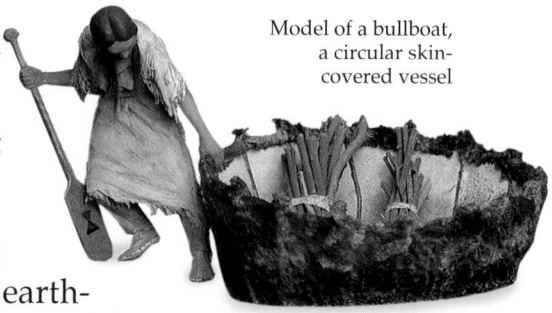

Model of a bullboat, a circular skin-covered vessel

FERTILE RIVER VALLEYS and open prairies, hot summers and numbingly cold winters – the Mandan and Hidatsa learned to adapt to and exploit their homeland on the upper Missouri River in North Dakota. They built permanent earth-lodge villages on the high banks above the river and farmed the bottom lands. Half of their food came from crops such as corn, the rest from the vital summer buffalo hunt. To deal with winter cold, they built separate lodges along the river, where there was plenty of wood for fuel. As hunter-farmers the Mandan and Hidatsa were typical of the prairie tribes, just as the Dakota were typical of the high plains tribes. They were fierce warriors, which was necessary to protect themselves from marauding bands of Dakota.

ACROSS THE RIVER
Settled on the Plains rivers, the Mandan used bullboats. Made from a (bull) buffalo hide stretched over a willow framework, a bullboat was light but strong enough to carry heavy loads. Able to move in very shallow water, it was usually a one-person craft. The paddler knelt in front and dipped the paddle straight down. To prevent the boat from spinning, the buffalo's tail was left on. Attached to a piece of wood, it acted as a stabilizer.

BRAIDED EARS
Raising crops was women's work, but men sometimes helped clear land or harvest the crops. A Plains woman, helped by her female kin, could farm 3 acres (1.2 ha) each year. She grew corn, beans, squash, sunflowers, and melon. Planting was done in spring and harvesting in September, when the ears of corn were husked (outer leaves of cobs removed). The best ears were braided into strings, hung up to dry, then stored in pits in the floor of the earth lodge.

INSIDE A MANDAN LODGE
In 1833–34 a German prince, Maximilian von Wied-Neuwied, toured the American West to study the tribes. To make a visual record of his findings, the prince took Swiss painter Karl Bodmer (1809–93) on the trip. They traveled far up the Missouri River and met the Mandan and Hidatsa tribes. Bodmer's painting (left) of the interior of a Mandan lodge shows warriors, with horses, dogs, and weapons to hand, viewed by the dim light of the chimney hole.

Chimney hole, covered by bullboat framework, lets in light

Roof of wooden rafters topped with willows, grass, and sod

CLOSE TO THE EARTH
Earth lodges were dome-shaped, up to 50 ft (15 m) wide. Built mainly by women, they were home to their extended families, together with horses, dogs, and belongings. An earth lodge was thought to be sacred, and its construction was accompanied by many ceremonies. All social activities and housekeeping took place around a central fireplace.

Entrance was a covered walkway with an inner skin door

Karl Bodmer's portrait of Four Bears – the last great Mandan chief

CHIEF FOUR BEARS
Prince Maximilian believed the Mandan were descendants of the Welsh prince Madoc, who supposedly sailed to America in 1170 – a tale long proved to be false! During the winter of 1833–34, so cold that his paints froze, Karl Bodmer produced several fine pictures, including this portrait of the Mandan chief Mato-Tope (Four Bears). Mato-Tope must have become used to posing for a portrait, since the artist George Catlin (1796–1872) had painted him the previous year.

INVALUABLE KNOWLEDGE
The story of the Hidatsa has been strikingly told by Buffalo Bird Woman (1839–1920s?) and her son, Edward Goodbird (1869–1938), who were photographed with Son of a Star (right) in 1906. Much of their story was related to an anthropologist (someone who studies cultures) working in collaboration with the American Museum of Natural History. Besides invaluable knowledge of tribal life and customs, their account detailed the move to a government reservation (1885–88) and the problems this brought.

MAKING PEMMICAN
Pemmican was the all-purpose emergency food of the Plains, with a very long shelf life. It was made by mixing dried buffalo meat, boiled fat, and chokecherries (bitter berries from local shrubs). For pounding the meat until it was nearly powder and for cracking the bones to boil out the fat, a large stone hammer was used. Pemmican was very nutritious and would keep for years.

A SIGN OF THE TINES
For weeding the fields of corn, the Hidatsa preferred rakes with deer antler tines (prongs). This was partly because they believed wooden rakes produced the worms that damaged the corn crop. Tribal stories told of deer weeding the garden of their ancestor, Eternal Grandmother, and of how she made the first rakes from their cast-off antlers.

War and peace

ON THE GREAT PLAINS, warfare was part of life but it rarely involved great battles between tribes. Instead, small bands of warriors made raids to steal horses or to avenge a death – and always to win honor. Audacity and courage were greatly respected and deeds were graded on a system of "coups" (the French word for blows), which included taking a scalp, stealing a horse, or touching an enemy in battle. War was a bloody and deadly business that inflicted serious casualties on each tribe. Tribal warfare was a test of personal courage and spiritual power, rather than a battle for territory and political control conducted by disciplined soldiers. Native North American war customs left them at a great disadvantage when fighting white and black regiments.

THE MASSACRE AT WOUNDED KNEE
In the turmoil created by the Ghost Dance (below left), on December 29, 1890, 470 7th Cavalry troopers were guarding 340 surrendered Sioux. A tense situation exploded and both sides opened fire. Over 64 soldiers and 200 Sioux (including unarmed women and children) were killed. The Sioux bodies were dumped into a mass grave. Wounded Knee became a symbol to Native North Americans of their mistreatment by whites.

Metal blade fitted around wooden handle

WAR PARTY
A Plains raiding party was armed with bows and arrows, shields, lances, clubs, and scalping knives. A war club might have a blade, spike, or shaped stone at the top. Tomahawk-pipes, like this Dakota example, were used more as prestigious ceremonial objects than as weapons.

Carved face is symbol of owner's supernatural helper, who appeared in Ghost Dance vision

Arapaho Ghost Dance wand

Wand made from wooden tube or hollow reed

Headdress is a circle of magpie and turkey feathers

Wand with white shaft and mottled feathers represents the female calumet

VISION OF HOPE
By the late 1800s, the Plains peoples, in despair on reservations, turned to a new ceremony, the Ghost Dancer. Born in a Paiute prophet's (Wovoka, pp. 40–41) vision, it promised the end of the whites and a return of the buffalo. Soon Ghost Dancers sought visions in which they visited the spirit world and met dead relatives. In later dances, they carried objects seen in the visions (left).

DOG SOCIETIES
Various Plains tribes, such as the Blackfeet, Hidatsa, and Gros Ventre, had a military Dog Society. On a tour of the West in 1833–34, Swiss artist Karl Bodmer painted this striking portrait of a Hidatsa Dog Dancer, Pehriska-Ruhpa (Two Ravens). Hidatsa Dogs were "contraries" and did everything backward – for example, if a warrior was meant to attack in battle, he was told to flee.

COMANCHE CHIEF
Such were the reputation and political skills of Quanah Parker (1845?–1911), war leader of the feared Comanche, that he became their first overall chief after peace in 1875. An outstanding politician, he worked with the U.S. government for the tribe's interests, getting better treatment for the Comanche on their Oklahoma reservation. He was also made a judge in the new Federal Court of Indian Offenses in Washington.

ON THE DEFENSIVE
Worn on the left arm, leaving hands free for weapons, a Plains warrior's shield was tough enough to stop an arrow or deflect a lance. A ritual of songs and prayers was involved in its construction, invoking protection by supernatural powers.

WAR OR PEACE?
Among the most sacred Plains objects were calumets. Calumets presented to another tribe guaranteed peace, because war could not be waged against relatives. The recipient of a calumet was promised long life, good fortune, and prosperity.

The Sun Dance

AT THE TIME of the summer buffalo hunt, when each tribe had reunited after scattering widely in the winter, most Plains peoples held the Sun Dance – the greatest of their ceremonies. The rites differed among tribes such as the Dakota, Crow, and Blackfeet, but the purpose was to thank the Great Spirit for past help and pray for future blessings. The ceremony fulfilled a promise by one person (a pledger) to show gratitude for aid from the spirit world, although it was for the benefit of the whole tribe. The ritual lasted several days and nights. Tribes built a sacred Sun Dance Lodge, where a sacred cottonwood tree, forked at the top, was at the center of the ceremony. Found by a warrior, it had been cut down by specially chosen virtuous women. The days of ritual dances ended with several kinds of ordeal. Volunteers chose to accept self-imposed pain in order to have a personal vision. It was also hoped that the Great Spirit would spare the whole tribe from future suffering.

Slow Bull, a Plains medicine man

Buffalo skull specially painted and placed at the altar of the Blackfeet Sun Dance

THE GREAT SPIRIT
The Plains world was filled with spirits who possessed power and inhabited places, persons, animals, even objects. Some tribes believed all power came from the Great Spirit. Individuals might sing to lesser spirits to plead for their aid, or by privation seek a vision that would transmit to them some sacred power. Those who gained great power became "medicine men," tribal leaders and advisers.

MOST POWERFUL MEDICINE
The Crow Sun Dance was held for someone seeking vengeance for the killing of a relative. A ceremonial doll was suspended by a hoop from the sacred cottonwood. Crow sacred stories tell of a warrior grieving for his family, who were killed by enemies. A vision showed him how to make the doll, which would ensure revenge.

Feather headdress decorated with fur and beads

Feather headdress adorning Dakota effigy

SACRED EFFIGIES
The Dakota attached special objects to the fork of the sacred cottonwood in the Sun Dance Lodge as the focus for a ritual dance. These objects, made of raw-hide, were effigies (symbolic figures). They were simple cut-out figures of a man (symbolizing the enemy) and a buffalo. The ritual ended with dancers firing arrows at the figures.

Crow deerskin doll is stuffed with sweetgrass

Simple buffalo effigy cut from a piece of rawhide

RESPECT FOR BUFFALO
As the vital resource at the center of their way of life, the buffalo was featured prominently by most Plains people in their versions of the Sun Dance. Both Blackfeet and Dakota painted buffalo skulls and decorated them with sage and grass.

Cylindrical case for storing the Blackfeet Natoas bundle, which included a sacred headdress

Digging stick

Eye and nose cavities were stuffed with sage and grass, as a symbolic offering to the buffalo to wish them successful grazing

Rawhide fringing

Detail from a painting by Frederic Remington (1861–1909)

AN AGONIZING ORDEAL
In the Sun Dance ordeal, all dancers fasted and endured privations. But some chose to have rawhide thongs driven through their chest muscles on wooden skewers and attached to the fork of the sacred cottonwood pole. Swaying to the music and blowing eagle-bone whistles, or even suspended from the fork, they gained release only when the skewers tore out of their flesh. Disturbed by this practice, the U.S. government banned the entire Sun Dance from 1904 to 1935.

A SACRED WOMAN
In addition to cutting down the sacred cottonwood tree, women sang during the various dances, brought the dancers presents, and took part in the ordeals. But most important, the Blackfeet ceremony depended on a Sacred Woman for the rituals. Whoever had pledged the Sun Dance had to buy a Natoas bundle, and it was transferred to the Sacred Woman in a special rite. Kept in a rawhide case, the Natoas bundle contained several sacred objects, such as face paints and rattles, but the most important were a headdress and a digging stick.

The high Plateau

THE GREAT PLATEAU, west of the northern Plains, was home to 25 tribes. It stretched from the Rockies westward to the Cascade Mountains of Oregon, and from the Fraser River south to Idaho and western Wyoming. Most tribes lived in tepee-like lodges in summer, and in winter, earth-covered, part-underground houses. Their main food was salmon and edible roots. Some tribes became traders and bartered skins, hemp, and horn bows for buffalo skins, superior robes, and decorated objects from the Plains. The Plateau peoples began using horses only in the 1700s but soon became famous for breeding and trading them. Trade brought prosperity, which ended only with pressure from white expansion after the 1830s.

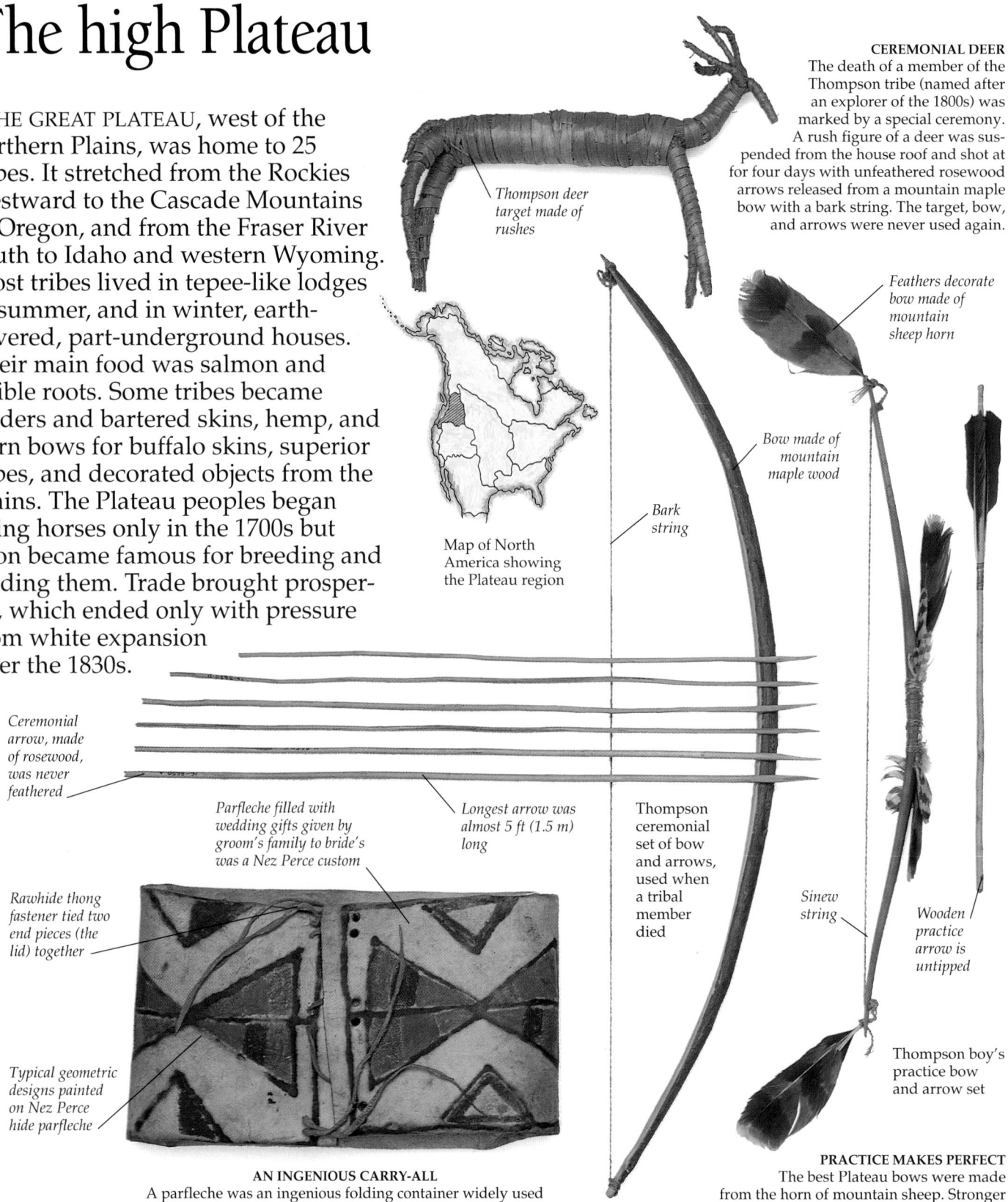

CEREMONIAL DEER
The death of a member of the Thompson tribe (named after an explorer of the 1800s) was marked by a special ceremony. A rush figure of a deer was suspended from the house roof and shot at for four days with unfeathered rosewood arrows released from a mountain maple bow with a bark string. The target, bow, and arrows were never used again.

AN INGENIOUS CARRY-ALL
A parfleche was an ingenious folding container widely used throughout the Plateau and Plains. Hung from a saddle, it was large enough to carry food (generally buffalo meat) and clothing. A strip of rawhide was folded and creased to make a base and two sides, then folded again one-third from each end. These end pieces were bent over to form a lid. Like other work with skins and hides, making parfleches was a task for women. Though the Nez Perce made their own, the Plateau tribes particularly valued parfleches from the Plains.

PRACTICE MAKES PERFECT
The best Plateau bows were made from the horn of mountain sheep. Stronger and more resilient than wood, sheep horn provided more thrust when the string was pulled, giving the arrows greater range and more accuracy. Boys were expected to develop their hunting skills very early; first shooting at stationary targets, then hunting small game such as rabbits. Plateau horn bows became important trade items, greatly valued by the Plains tribes, who thought them much superior to their own.

THE GREAT CHASE
Clashes with whites escalated into the Nez Perce War of 1877. The band of Chief Joseph (c. 1840–1904) fought a series of running battles with increasingly larger forces of the U.S. Cavalry and local volunteers. The Nez Perce consistently outfought their enemies in a chase lasting four months and covering over 1,600 miles (2,600 km), until they were forced to surrender only 30 miles (48 km) short of sanctuary in Canada.

Chief Joseph

Red and black geometric design appliquéd to Thompson hide saddlebag

A REVOLUTION
The horse revolutionized the Plateau peoples' way of life. It extended the range of their summer migrations and spread their trade down into California and deep into the Plains. As a result, they brought back not only bartered goods but many of their neighbors' customs. However, they did not adopt the Plains travois for transport. Instead they used pack saddles and saddlebags, such as this double one from the Thompson tribe, who lived in southern British Columbia.

Antler spike

RAIDING PARTY
The Thompson tribe used to raid their neighbors for booty, revenge, and honor, much like most Native North American peoples. This two-handed war club is crudely decorated, showing a lake with three warriors nearby. The notches at each end were probably ornamental but may have been for tallying numbers of enemy killed, just as Western gunfighters were alleged to notch their guns.

Thompson birchwood war club, also used for hunting beaver

Hide fringing

Each notch perhaps denoted an enemy or beaver that had been killed with this club

IN THE BAG
The Nez Perce were famous for their cornhusk bags. Made of twisted hemp fiber, twined without using a loom, the bags were decorated with cords made from the inner parts of cornhusks. Cords were dyed with colors made of natural materials to produce typical geometric designs, with a different design appearing on the reverse side of the bag. Flexible, flat containers, cornhusk bags were used to carry foodstuffs, roots, and berries. After horses, they were the Nez Perce's most important trade goods.

The Great Basin

Map of North America showing the Great Basin – Nevada, Utah, Idaho, Oregon, Wyoming, and Colorado

A BAKING DESERT IN SUMMER, lashed by storms and snow in winter, the Great Basin has always had meager resources. Nine tribes, scattered over 400,000 sq miles (1 million sq km), had adapted so well to their environment that their way of life endured for some 10,000 years. Without agriculture, and living on wild foods ranging from insects and seeds to lizards and deer, the ingenuity of these migratory people is easy to miss. They needed no permanent homes, as they migrated with the seasons, gathering in large encampments during pine nut harvests and rabbit drives. After gold was discovered here in 1859, their lives changed drastically.

PAIUTE PROPHET
In 1888 a Nevada Paiute shaman, Wovoka (white name Jack Wilson, 1856?–1932), began to prophesy that by using a new ceremony (the Ghost Dance, which spread rapidly to the Plains), the white man would be swept away, the buffalo returned, and the old ways restored. Though his message stressed nonviolence, the white authorities reacted with brutality.

Nevada Washoe basket-maker Datsolali (white name, Louisa Keyser)

FAMOUS BASKET WEAVER
The Great Basin tribes were expert basket weavers, particularly the Washoe, whose products were greatly valued by white buyers. Datsolali (1835?–1925) was the most famous of all Native American basket weavers. Her baskets showed control of difficult shapes and displayed traditional patterns involving extrafine stitching.

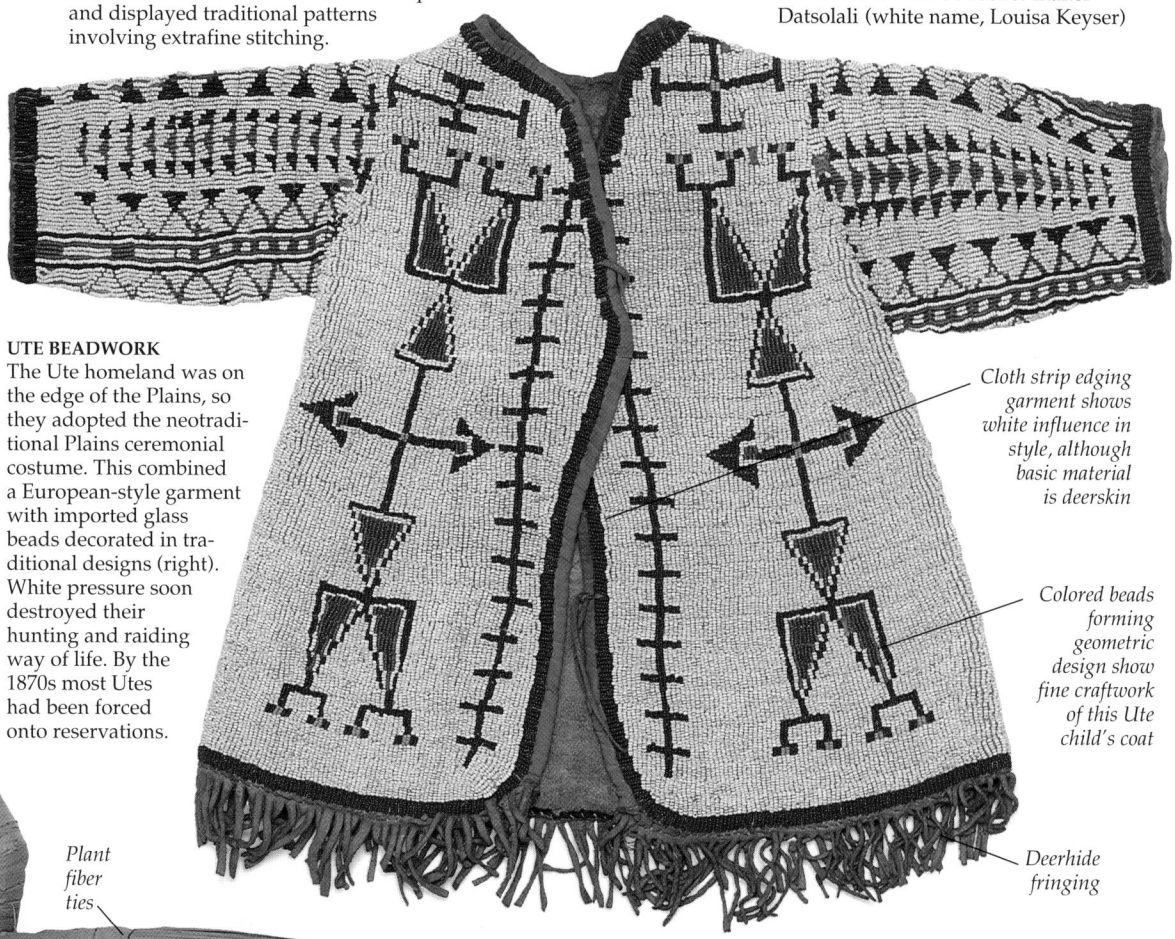

UTE BEADWORK
The Ute homeland was on the edge of the Plains, so they adopted the neotraditional Plains ceremonial costume. This combined a European-style garment with imported glass beads decorated in traditional designs (right). White pressure soon destroyed their hunting and raiding way of life. By the 1870s most Utes had been forced onto reservations.

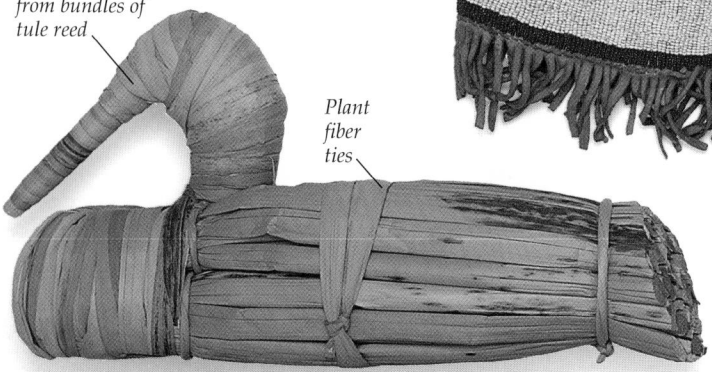

DUCK DECOY
The Northern Paiute of northwestern Nevada hunted any game available, including rabbits and marmots. In the spring, migrating birds, such as ducks, were hunted with the help of duck-shaped decoys made from bulrush (tule) bundles tied together with rush fiber. Floating realistically on reed marshes within range of the hidden hunters' bows, they convinced the ducks it was safe to land.

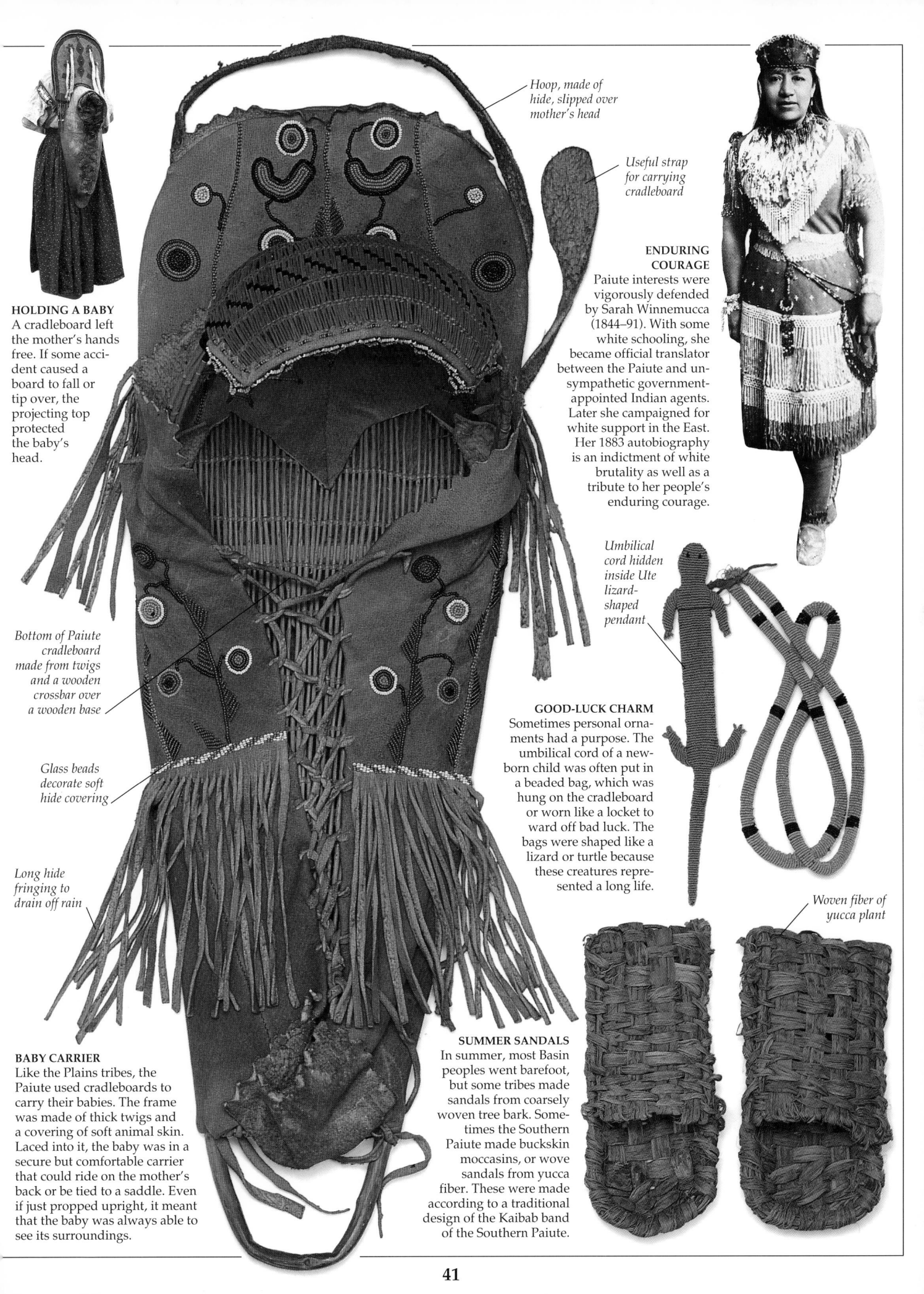

HOLDING A BABY
A cradleboard left the mother's hands free. If some accident caused a board to fall or tip over, the projecting top protected the baby's head.

ENDURING COURAGE
Paiute interests were vigorously defended by Sarah Winnemucca (1844–91). With some white schooling, she became official translator between the Paiute and unsympathetic government-appointed Indian agents. Later she campaigned for white support in the East. Her 1883 autobiography is an indictment of white brutality as well as a tribute to her people's enduring courage.

GOOD-LUCK CHARM
Sometimes personal ornaments had a purpose. The umbilical cord of a newborn child was often put in a beaded bag, which was hung on the cradleboard or worn like a locket to ward off bad luck. The bags were shaped like a lizard or turtle because these creatures represented a long life.

BABY CARRIER
Like the Plains tribes, the Paiute used cradleboards to carry their babies. The frame was made of thick twigs and a covering of soft animal skin. Laced into it, the baby was in a secure but comfortable carrier that could ride on the mother's back or be tied to a saddle. Even if just propped upright, it meant that the baby was always able to see its surroundings.

SUMMER SANDALS
In summer, most Basin peoples went barefoot, but some tribes made sandals from coarsely woven tree bark. Sometimes the Southern Paiute made buckskin moccasins, or wove sandals from yucca fiber. These were made according to a traditional design of the Kaibab band of the Southern Paiute.

Californian hunter-gatherers

Map of North America showing the California region

NATIVE AMERICANS found California as attractive in the 1760s as their American successors did in the 1960s. The reasons were simple. Except for the southeastern desert, the climate and resources made life easy. Warfare was rare and farming almost unknown, the people preferring to be hunter-gatherers. Isolated by deserts and mountains from the warlike tribes to the east, the 50 tribes lived on fish and game, but seeds (especially acorns) played a major role in their diet. Their ceremonies petitioned the spirit world to ensure food and health. The arrival in 1769 of the Spanish, establishing missions in the south, began the erosion of this way of life, and the Gold Rush of 1849 in the north destroyed it.

THE MODOC WAR
In 1864, Kintpuash (Captain Jack) led a group of Modoc who refused to accept their new reservation, resulting in the Modoc War of 1872. The U.S. Army besieged Kintpuash and 80 men for six months near Tule Lake. After violating a peace parley, Kintpuash surrendered and was hanged.

FEATHER BUNCH
The Maidu, nicknamed "Digger Indians" by the Europeans (because they searched for edible roots to supplement their acorn diet), lived in partly underground dwellings, up to 40 ft (12 m) across. At some of their ceremonies, both men and women wore feather bunches (right).

Maidu dance plume, or bunch (worn on crown of head), made of quills, feathers, wood, and string

Single piece of curved wood forms basic frame of Pomo flail

Elaborate design on ceramic doll echoes tattoo designs on a Mohave warrior

Closely woven netting made of willow

DESERT PEOPLE
The Mohave, typical of the Yuman tribes along the lower Colorado River, farmed the bottom land, relying on the annual flooding of the river for raising crops. By the late 1800s, confined to a reservation, they were selling souvenirs, like these ceramic dolls (above), at a nearby railroad station.

GATHERING SEEDS
The Pomo lived between the ocean and the Coast Range. Their dwellings, each home to several families, were 30-ft (9-m) -long pole frameworks covered with thatch. They were expert hunters and fishermen, but the most important part of their diet was acorns, ground into meal. They also ate seeds, roots, and berries. Women used flails (right) to knock seeds into a collecting, or burden, basket.

CEREMONIAL FEATHER CROWN
The Maidu of California's Central Valley wore elaborate feather decorations for their ceremonial dances. In a dance called *lo'li*, only the women took part. They sometimes wore feather bunches (far left), but always an elaborate feather crown called an *unu'ni*. Men alone participated in the dance that followed, and they also wore the *unu'ni* crown (above).

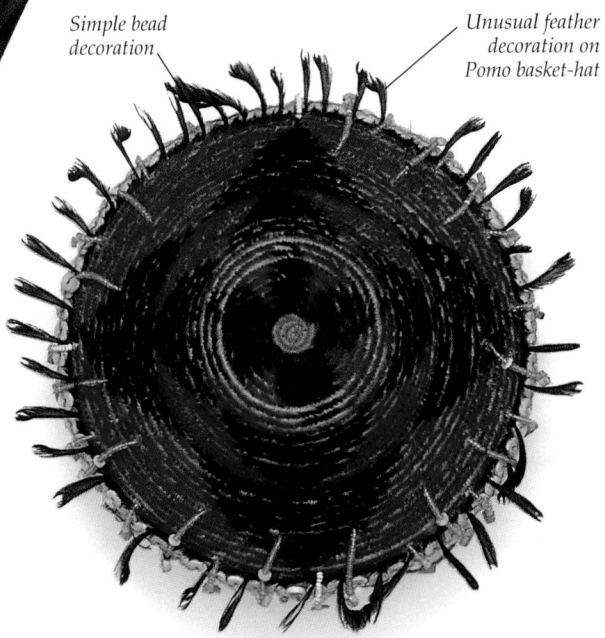

BASKETRY HAT WITH FEATHERWORK
The Pomo are widely regarded as outstanding basketmakers. Unlike most Native North American peoples, Pomo men as well as women wove baskets. Employing four or more materials, some for working in colored patterns, the weavers used both the coiling technique and four different kinds of twining. Particularly unusual was the idea of decorating the baskets by attaching brightly colored feathers to the surface.

THE LAST OF THE YAHI
In 1911 the last survivor of the isolated Yahi tribe, long believed to have died out, appeared in a northern California town. He was "adopted" by anthropologists at the University of California, who wished to learn about his way of life. They named him Ishi (Yahi for "man"). Ishi died of tuberculosis in 1916.

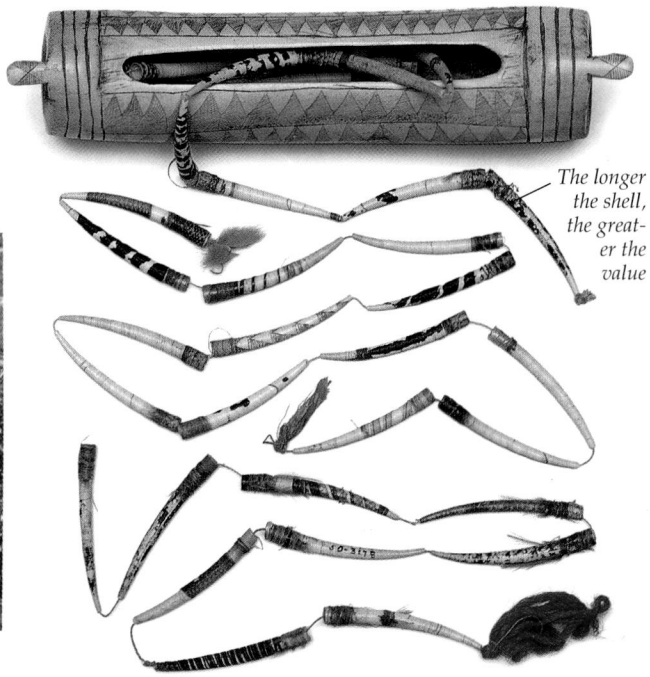

SPENDING MONEY
Far to the north, on Vancouver Island, strings of dentalium shells (above) were highly valued ornaments. Brought south by traders of the Tolowa tribe, they were used as a form of money by many of the California peoples. But the Pomo preferred to make a rival currency from the white mineral magnesite, or from clamshells. Most Northern tribes made purses from elk antlers (top), which were strikingly decorated.

The stunning Southwest

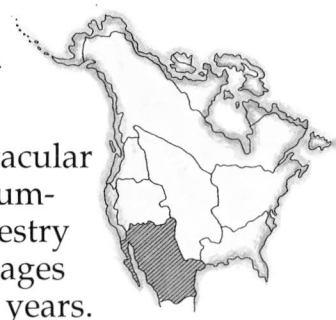

Map of North America showing the Southwest region

THE SOUTHWEST IS A LAND of great majesty and spectacular contrasts, of mountain and desert, scorching heat in summer and cold in winter. Its peoples can trace their ancestry back 2,000 years, and some of their stone and clay villages have been continuously occupied for more than 1,000 years. In this arid land, the Pueblo peoples learned to irrigate their crops with the little water available. Their rituals were closely connected with persuading the beings of the spirit world to bring rain. So, too, were those of the Papago of the desert to the south. Though not warriors, Pueblos sometimes fought each other and defended themselves against Navajo and Apache.

Painted wood Zuni lightning symbol set up on a kiva altar

PRAYING FOR RAIN
Both Zuni and Hopi Pueblo peoples lived bounded by rituals that connected them to the spirit world. Every August the Hopi held a nine-day Snake Ceremonial to bring the rain that ensured a good harvest. Snake sticks (symbols of the lightning that comes with rain) were set up on a kiva altar. At the ritual's end, painted dancers held live snakes in their mouths, then released them into the desert.

Bird-animal design on coiled basketry Havasupai bowl

PEACEFUL LIFE IN AN ISOLATED CANYON
For nearly 900 years the Havasupai have farmed Cataract Canyon in Arizona, using skills learned from the Hopi and irrigating with water from the Colorado River. Isolated in the canyon, they have no tradition of warfare.

Typical geometric decoration

Unusual effigy of a tattooed woman shapes this Papago pottery vessel

PAPAGO POTS
Like their cousins the Pima, the Papago were descended from the Hohokam people, who lived more than 2,000 years ago in settled villages along what is now Arizona's border with Mexico. In tribal life, men were responsible for raising the usual crops of squash, corn, and beans while women wove baskets and made pots.

Desert frog was inspiration for bowl's decoration

Traditional black geometric design on a light background

Four step-shaped corners, modeled after frogs, decorate this large, elaborate Zuni bowl, which once belonged to a rain priest

ANCIENT ART
The Pueblo tradition of pottery making stretches back to their ancient ancestors in the region. Styles in design vary among the Pueblos but are always highly decorated in traditional colors of red, black, and white, with geometric or representational designs.

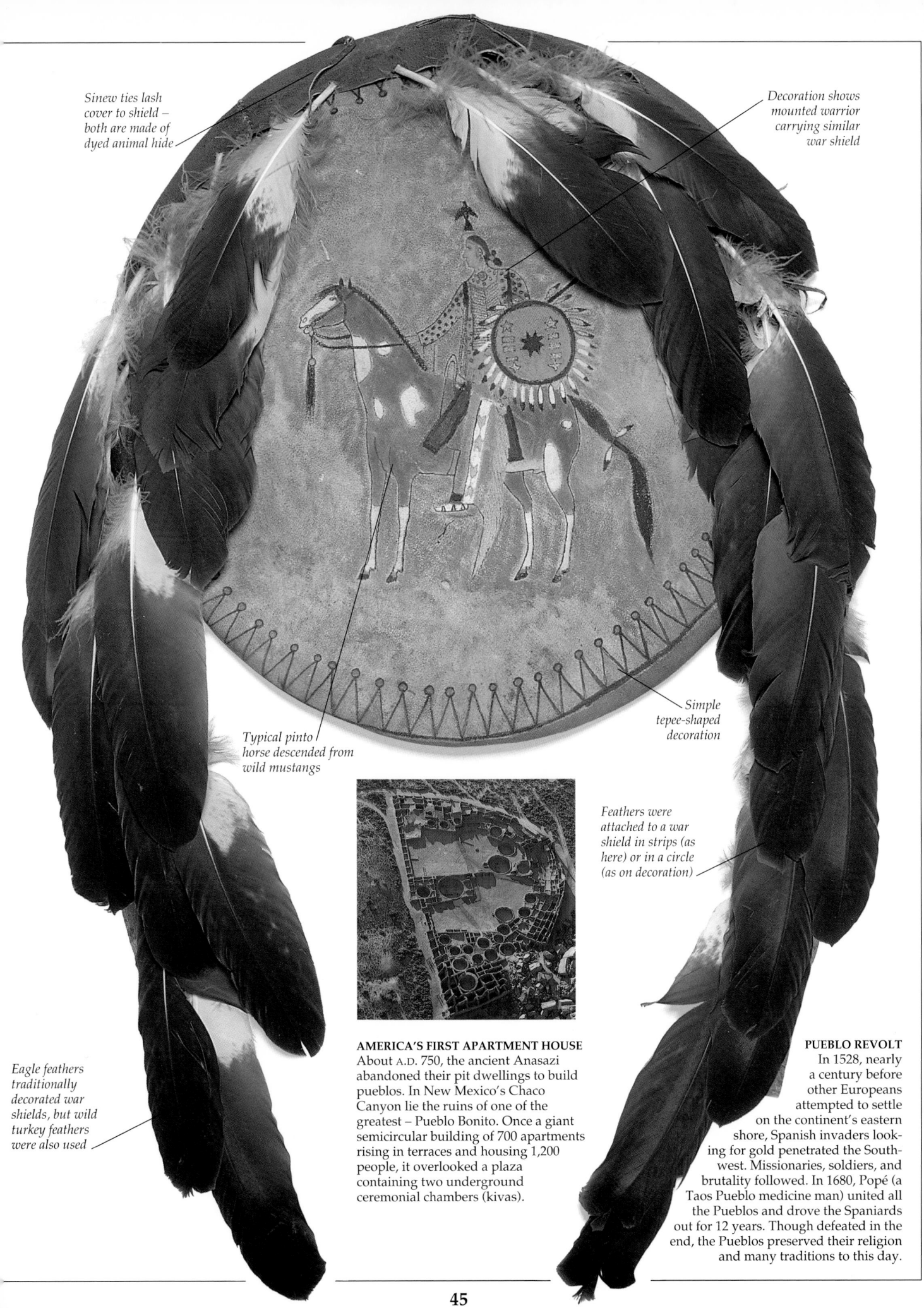

AMERICA'S FIRST APARTMENT HOUSE
About A.D. 750, the ancient Anasazi abandoned their pit dwellings to build pueblos. In New Mexico's Chaco Canyon lie the ruins of one of the greatest – Pueblo Bonito. Once a giant semicircular building of 700 apartments rising in terraces and housing 1,200 people, it overlooked a plaza containing two underground ceremonial chambers (kivas).

PUEBLO REVOLT
In 1528, nearly a century before other Europeans attempted to settle on the continent's eastern shore, Spanish invaders looking for gold penetrated the Southwest. Missionaries, soldiers, and brutality followed. In 1680, Popé (a Taos Pueblo medicine man) united all the Pueblos and drove the Spaniards out for 12 years. Though defeated in the end, the Pueblos preserved their religion and many traditions to this day.

The Pueblo peoples

PASSING THE TEST
Hopi girls were judged fit for marriage after passing tests of women's skills. Then they were allowed to style their hair in complicated squash blossom coils.

AMAZING BIRD
From about A.D. 500 the Anasazi, people of the Southwest, created small pottery figures of birds and animals. Remarkably similar figures were produced by Zuni potters 1300 years later (above).

ON THE WINDSWEPT TABLETOP ROCKS towering above the desert and along the Southwest's few rivers stand stone and adobe settlements. Today Native Americans inhabit some 30 villages from the Rio Grande to northern Arizona. The first Spanish explorers called the inhabitants Pueblo (village) people, but they were not a single tribe. The villages were independent and the people (including Hopi and Zuni) spoke different languages. From early times they have raised crops of squash, beans, and corn. Their lives are guided by kachinas, spirit beings who enter the bodies of selected men wearing masks and performing sacred dances. Men also govern the community, but women own all property which is inherited by their daughters.

CEREMONIAL BOWS AND ARROWS
On June 26 (five days after the summer solstice) the Hopi begin an elaborate ceremony called Niman. It is held to ensure a successful harvest. For 16 days, solemn rituals and prayers for rain mark the return of the kachinas to the spirit world. The departing kachinas offer the villagers symbolic gifts, including ears of corn and bows and arrows (far left).

Natural pigment decorates wooden rabbit stick

Narrow strips of sinew glued to back of wooden bow for extra strength

BOOMERANG THAT ISN'T
In the fall and winter, rabbit hunting is both a sport and a ritual ceremony for the Hopi community. A mile-round circle of hunters contracts until rabbits can be hit with throwing sticks (left).The sticks are curved and often decorated. They strike like boomerangs but don't return when they miss.

Wooden kachina doll represents Aholi, who accompanies the Chief Hopi Kachina

FAMOUS POTTERY
For 900 years Pueblo peoples have developed a highly individual style of decorated pottery. San Ildefonso Pueblo traditionally produced geometric designs in two colors. Here, in 1919, Julian Martinez invented a matte-black-on-polished-black design for pots made by his wife, Maria.

Nakachok, a painted wooden Hopi kachina doll

NOT A TOY
Kachina dolls were not toys but a vital part of the education of every Pueblo child. These dolls, specially carved to represent the different types of kachina, taught children about the appearance and roles of the many kachinas. Kachina-doll carving was most highly developed by the Hopi and Zuni.

Nataska, a Hopi kachina doll, helps discipline erring children

BEJEWELED
Famous for their beautiful jewelry, the Navajo decorated this leather wrist guard in their typical style, with silver and turquoise.

Apache and Navajo

THE ARID MOUNTAINS and deserts of the Southwest became home to the Apache and Navajo, who may have migrated south from the far Northwest in the 1400s. Hunters and warriors, they raided first their Pueblo neighbors and later the colonizing Spanish pushing north from Mexico. From both they learned important agricultural skills. The Navajo combined sheep raising, farming, and raiding until local American forces under Kit Carson (1809–68) forced their surrender in 1864. Rebuilding their way of life, they added silverwork to their arts. Some Apache, learning from the Pueblo villagers, took up farming, but most remained hunter-raiders. Feared by other tribes and by Europeans as the fiercest warriors in the Southwest, they faced their final defeat in the mid-1880s.

BRAVE WARRIOR
Geronimo (1829–1909) was his Mexican name; his Apache name (Goyanthlay) meant "the Yawner." He became the most famous Apache warrior and fought the American invasion of Apache lands in the 1860s and 1870s. He was caught in 1877 and confined on the San Carlos reservation in Arizona. On his escape in 1881, he resumed raiding – to the terror of both Mexican and American settlers. He was photographed (above, far right) just before he finally surrendered in 1886.

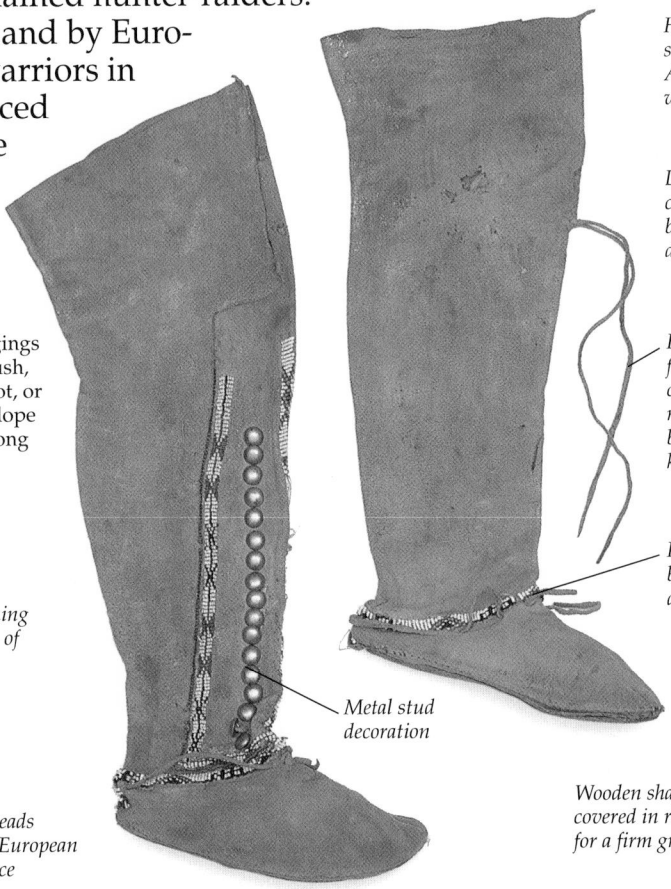

BEST FOOT FORWARD
As an alternative to wearing moccasins with separate hide leggings to protect their legs from thornbrush, Apaches wore a one-piece soft boot, or "long moccasin," made from antelope skin or deerskin. Usually, men's long moccasins reached to just below the knee, while those of women extended above it.

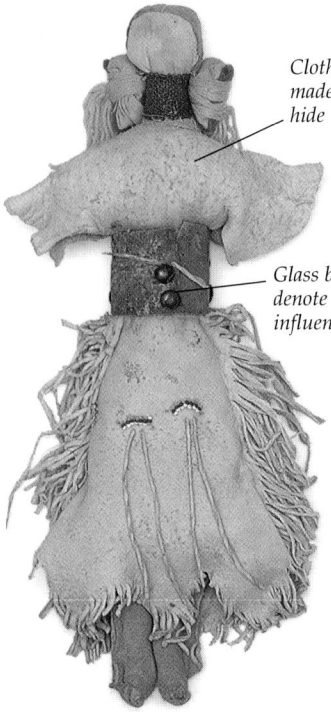

FAVORITE DOLL
Toys of Apache children, like those of children everywhere, imitated the adult world into which they would grow. This rag doll has its hair arranged in the Hopi style worn by an unmarried girl. When an Apache girl entered puberty, a four-day ceremony was held. Ritual singing alternated with feasting. Like the Hopi girls, an Apache girl was taught her future responsibilities by an older woman and ran a ritual race to prove her strength and courage. After this, she was ready for marriage.

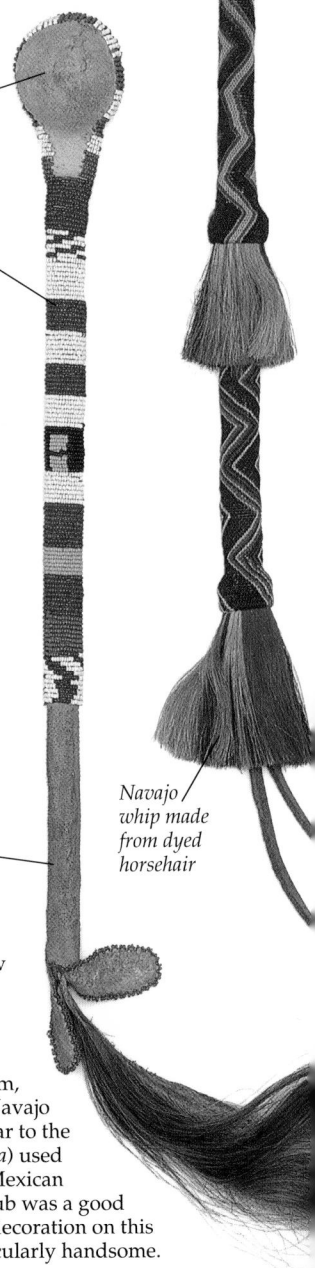

INTO BATTLE!
Like all Native Americans, the Navajo and Apache knew nothing of horses until they met Spanish colonists with their mounts in the 1500s. However, they quickly learned to use and breed them, especially for warfare. The Navajo whip (far right) is very similar to the quirt (from the Spanish *cuerta*) used by American cowboys and Mexican *vaqueros*. The Apache war club was a good close-quarter weapon – the decoration on this example (near right) is particularly handsome.

Upper bar

Shed rod

Colored wool yarn

Wood batten separates upright threads

Comb beats cross-threads into place

Motifs evolved since the 1870s, including diamond shapes

A TRADITIONAL WEAVE
Navajo beliefs tell how Spider Woman (one of their Holy People and a spirit being) first taught women how to weave. Skills are passed down from mother to daughter in a tradition that has lasted for generations. Tools were often handed on, like the batten to separate the warp (up-thread) and the comb to beat in place the weft (cross-thread). All property in Navajo clans passed from mother to daughter.

Tassel decoration made of hide

Wool attaches woven rug to lower bar

BEAUTIFULLY WOVEN
The Navajo first learned weaving skills in the late 1600s from the Pueblo peoples, using wool from sheep originally raided from the Spanish. By the mid-1800s, Navajo textiles were traded all over the West. Blankets were woven in intricate patterns and traditional colors, which changed over time. From the late 1800s, American merchants encouraged the weaving of rugs with pictorial designs, like the one above. This form of Navajo art is now well known and valued worldwide.

Beaded Apache tobacco pouch fringed with metal decoration

Cow's-tail attachment, dyed red

FINE BEADWORK
The Apache did not become known for pottery like the Hopi, nor for weaving and silverwork like the Navajo. Apache women, however, made beautiful baskets of willow rods and did fine beadwork, as shown in this elaborate tobacco pouch.

Papago and Pima

IN THE PARCHED DESERTS of what is now Arizona and northern Mexico, over 2,000 years ago the Hohokam people built irrigation systems to raise crops. Their descendants are the Pima and Papago (the Papagos' name for themselves, O'Odham, means "the People"). Using this inherited knowledge of river irrigation, the Pima settled in villages by the Salt and Gila rivers, raising corn, squash, and beans, and adding wheat around 1700. Their surplus of food became so large, they supplied California miners and, during the Civil War, the Union Army. The desert-dwelling Papago had to rely on seasonal flood water for farming and so stayed seminomadic. From the fermented fruit of the saguaro cactus they made wine to be used in rituals. Both tribes had similar ceremonies and both worshiped two main divine beings – Elder Brother and Earthmaker.

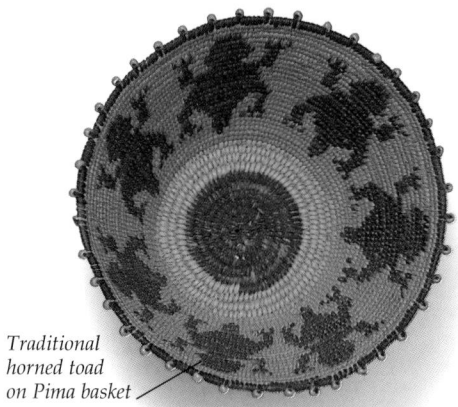

Traditional horned toad on Pima basket

ENDLESS USES
As nearly unbreakable containers, baskets had endless uses. Bowl-shaped ones were used for storing corn and shallow ones for carrying fruit collected from the top of the saguaro cactus. Designs picturing animals began to emerge in the 1800s.

THE ART OF BASKETMAKING
Basketmaking became an art among the Pima. Traditional techniques involved close coils of willow wound around bulrushes. Patterns were produced by adding pieces of the black devil's claw plant to make a striking contrast. Papago basketry also borrowed from Spanish designs. A basket was sometimes so large that the maker had to climb inside to finish it!

BRIDLE WEAR
The Papago were seminomadic, with few water resources. Horses were useful for traveling between their summer field villages in the desert and their winter well villages near mountain springs.

Feather-decorated hide covers this Papago wooden shield

MOCK BATTLES
Papago and Pima ceremonies included mock battles in which shields like this one were used. Though not fierce raiders like the Apache, they found war with other tribes was often unavoidable and were effective and successful warriors. In the Civil War, the Pima defended Arizona on behalf of the Union, defeating Confederate forces. After 1865 they served as valued scouts for the army in its campaigns against the Apache.

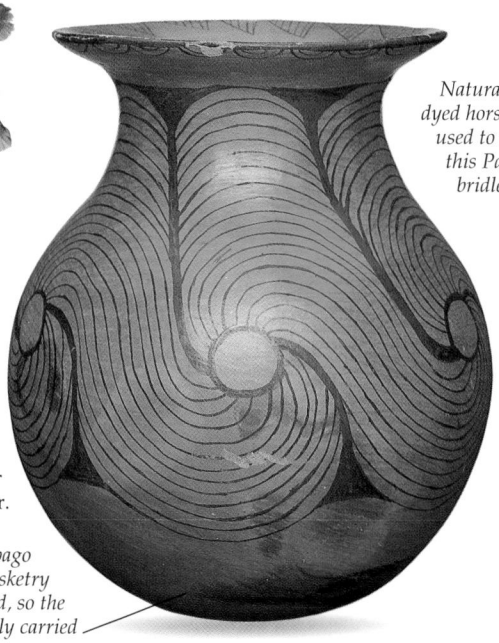

SIMPLE BUT EXQUISITE
Like the other peoples of the Southwest, the Pima and Papago were potters. Compared with the Hopi and Zuni, however, their designs were much simpler.

Rounded bottom of this Papago pottery water jar fits into a basketry ring worn on top of the head, so the jar could be easily carried

Natural and dyed horsehair used to make this Papago bridle rein

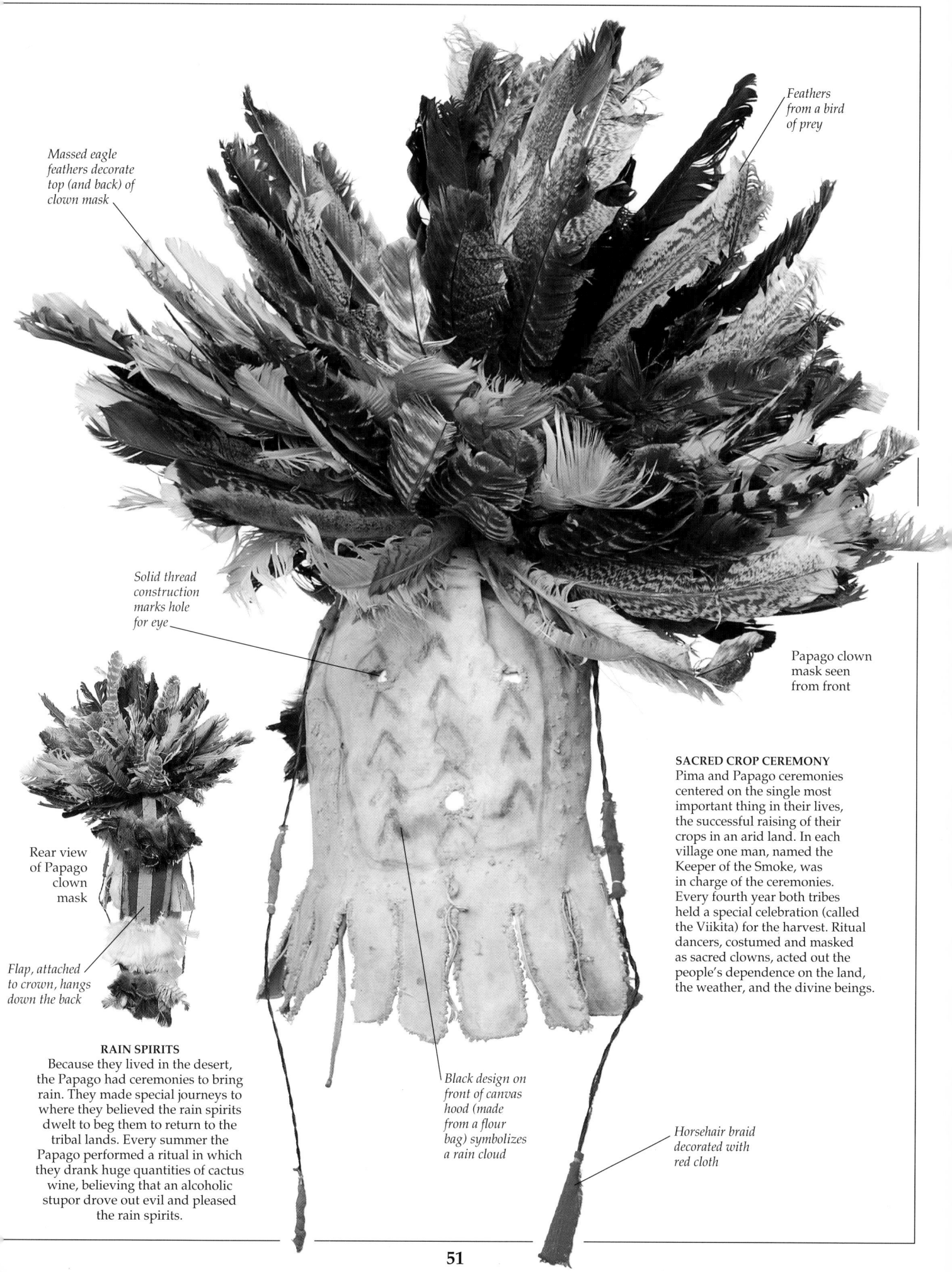

SACRED CROP CEREMONY
Pima and Papago ceremonies centered on the single most important thing in their lives, the successful raising of their crops in an arid land. In each village one man, named the Keeper of the Smoke, was in charge of the ceremonies. Every fourth year both tribes held a special celebration (called the Viikita) for the harvest. Ritual dancers, costumed and masked as sacred clowns, acted out the people's dependence on the land, the weather, and the divine beings.

RAIN SPIRITS
Because they lived in the desert, the Papago had ceremonies to bring rain. They made special journeys to where they believed the rain spirits dwelt to beg them to return to the tribal lands. Every summer the Papago performed a ritual in which they drank huge quantities of cactus wine, believing that an alcoholic stupor drove out evil and pleased the rain spirits.

Land of the totem poles

BETWEEN THE DARK FORESTS and the ocean's edge in the rainy Northwest, there grew an extraordinary culture almost untouched by Europeans until the late 1700s. The people of this area, divided into about 30 tribes, never developed agriculture, but were able to live comfortably from the teeming riches of the sea, the forest, and the rivers that filled with salmon during their annual runs. The bountiful environment allowed development of a splendid art and a complex society of nobles, commoners, and slaves. Wealthy families, proud of their status, expressed it in sumptuous ceremonies and monumental artworks, especially the towering wood totem poles.

Map of North America showing the Northwest region

Raven above a bear

Abalone-inlaid ivory handle

Hide strap used to lash knife to wrist

Iron blade of Tlingit fighting knife

WAR PARTIES
Northwest Coast warfare was typically a quick raid, either for revenge or to acquire plunder and slaves. The northernmost tribes also waged wars to drive away neighboring enemy tribes and control their land. Warriors wore wooden helmets and body armor made from strips of wood joined with rawhide. Weapons were bows, clubs, and knives (above). War knives originally had blades of stone or bone, later of traded iron. Knives were lashed to the wrist during battle.

Elegantly carved fins on Haida halibut club

HOOKED ON HALIBUT
The island-dwelling Haida relied on fishing. Halibut were caught by setting hooks close to the ocean bed. Once hauled to the surface, such fish had to be stunned with clubs immediately – at up to 400 lb (180 kg), their struggles might upset the canoe. The canoe was dug out of the trunk of a giant cedar and its prow decorated with an elaborate abstract carving.

Carving on the upper part of this Haida totem pole represents a raven

Intricate carving adorns this model of a Haida tomb

PERIOD OF MOURNING
A dead Haida was mourned ceremonially at home for a period of four to six days. The body was then placed in a grave box and taken out of the house through a specially made exit. The remains were put in a grave house, perhaps as large as an ordinary home, and commemorated with a memorial post.

TOTEM POLE VILLAGE
Architecture was one of the great achievements of the Northwest Coast peoples. The huge wooden houses had walls of cedar planks fitted over a massive cedar framework. They were designed by architects who supervised skilled artisans and gangs of laborers, often slaves from other tribes. Several related families lived in a house. Living space reflected rank, the highest place of honor being the back wall. A forest of totem poles dotted the village. Some were built into the fronts of houses, with holes at their bases for door openings. Free-standing poles were often memorials.

A FAMILY'S STATUS
Totem poles were not idols, as Christian missionaries believed, but monuments proclaiming a family's status by recording its family tree. Every household claimed through its legends a relationship with a spirit being in the form of a noble animal such as a raven, wolf, bear, or eagle. Carvings representing these beings were family crests, much like coats of arms in medieval Europe.

SMOKING PIPES
Tlingit men never smoked until they obtained tobacco from white traders, c. 1800. Then they began to produce an astonishing variety of intricately carved wooden pipes with metal bowls, used only by men – women did not smoke. Designs depicted crests. This Tlingit pipe has two carved and painted wooden wolves and is inlaid with abalone shells.

SECRETS BEHIND TOTEM POLES
Wealthy families commissioned sculptors to carve totem poles for various purposes, mostly related to burial rites and memorials to the dead. The heir of a deceased chief might erect a pole in the chief's honor as part of the process of taking over his role and titles. Sometimes a dead chief's remains were interred in a box on top of the pole. Raising a totem pole was always accompanied by a great ceremony: the potlatch (pp. 56–57).

Art second to none

IN THE FLICKERING FIRELIGHT of a Northwest house during the winter ceremonies, two great arts were dramatically displayed together – ritual dances and intricately carved masks. The dances, held by secret societies to initiate a new member, enacted the links between ancestors and spirit beings. Masked dancers represented the power and continuing presence of the spirit world. The ceremony was both ritual and theater, for the dancers used spectacular special effects to enhance the story they were telling. Membership in a society, the right to dance, and the possession of masks helped define privileges in this status-conscious culture. Both male and female shamans also wore ritual masks in their role as doctors.

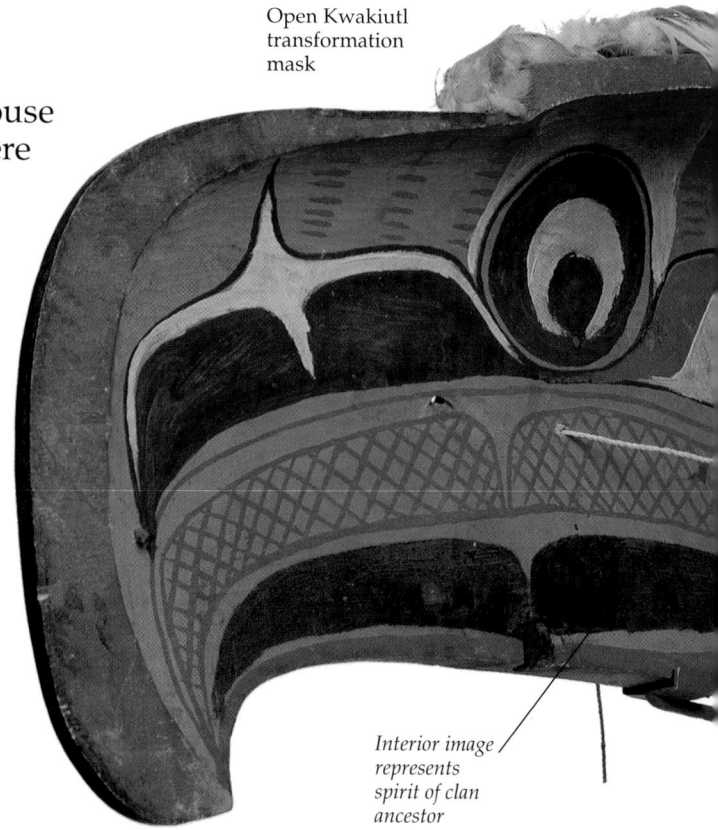

Open Kwakiutl transformation mask

Interior image represents spirit of clan ancestor

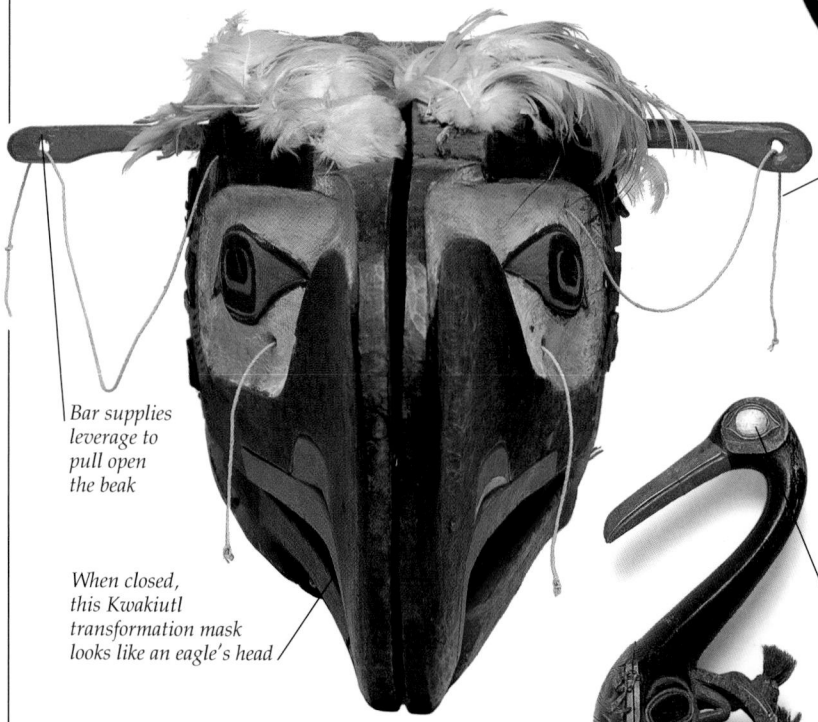

Cord, looping through eye and cheekbones, is pulled to open up the mask

Bar supplies leverage to pull open the beak

When closed, this Kwakiutl transformation mask looks like an eagle's head

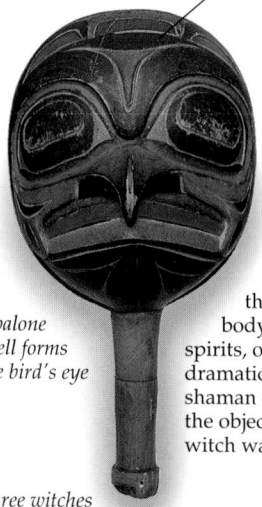

Haida wooden rattle in form of a hawk

SHAMAN'S RATTLES
Shamans were revered by the tribe for their awesome powers. These derived from special access to the spirit world through a personal guardian spirit, summoned by singing and the shaking of a sacred rattle. Illness was thought to be caused by the intrusion of a small object into the body or by the loss or theft of the soul by spirits, often manipulated by witches. In a dramatic ceremony performed for a fee, a shaman cured the sick person by removing the object or by restoring the lost soul. The witch was then identified and punished.

Abalone shell forms the bird's eye

Three witches planning evil activities are guarded by an octopus (near handle)

Tlingit shaman's wooden oyster catcher rattle

Dead man with protruding tongue in bill of kingfisher

Red ball is the Sun, once stolen; raven is now releasing it to light up the world

Tlingit wooden raven rattle

SECRET SOCIETIES
The Kwakiutl, who probably began the secret societies that eventually spread across the Northwest, had three: the Shaman Society, representing violent and threatening spirits; the Dluwulaxa, linked to the sky spirits; and the Nutlam, whose ancestor was the wolf spirit. Most important to the Shaman Society was a cannibal spirit – the dancers in this ceremony, called Hamatsa, had great prestige and wore particularly elaborate masks. Starting in mid-November the Kwakiutls held Winter Rituals for four months to establish a connection between uninitiated youths and a particular supernatural being, after which the youths became members of the appropriate secret society.

BEHIND THE MASK
Separate from the winter ceremonies were dances that displayed the household's privileges. This spectacular Kwakiutl transformation mask (changing from a bird's face to a human one) was probably part of such a dance. It was fixed to the dancer's head by a frame of wickerwork and animal sinews. The two bars at the back were linked by draw cords to the sides of the beak, and a third cord led to the lower part of the beak. Manipulating the cords instantly transformed an eagle spirit into one with a fierce human face.

RED AS THE SUN
The Bella Coola lived in northern British Columbia, Canada, between two groups of the Kwakiutl. Membership in their Dance Society, usually hereditary, was a coveted privilege because it brought great status. At their four-night winter ceremony, members performed dances taught to them by the spirit beings of the sky. Wearing spherical masks, such as the Spirit of the Sun (at right), the dancers acted out with great drama the central stories of the tribe's beliefs. Masks were designed for a striking effect rather than a readily identifiable spirit.

The power of potlatch

IN THE NORTHWEST, gaining wealth brought the possibility of status, but in the great potlatch ceremonies, giving wealth away guaranteed it. Potlatches were lavish distributions of gifts from host to guests, who might number in the hundreds. They took place in order to gain acceptance for a change in status or the acquisition of privileges. Potlatches did not bankrupt the giver. Being host at one potlatch guaranteed being a guest – and therefore a receiver of gifts – at others. In a society of often intense rivalries, potlatches siphoned off the tensions that otherwise might have led to war. Potlatches are still held today. A Canadian government ban, from 1884 to 1951, was defied by the Kwakiutl, and there has been a general revival of the ceremony since the 1960s.

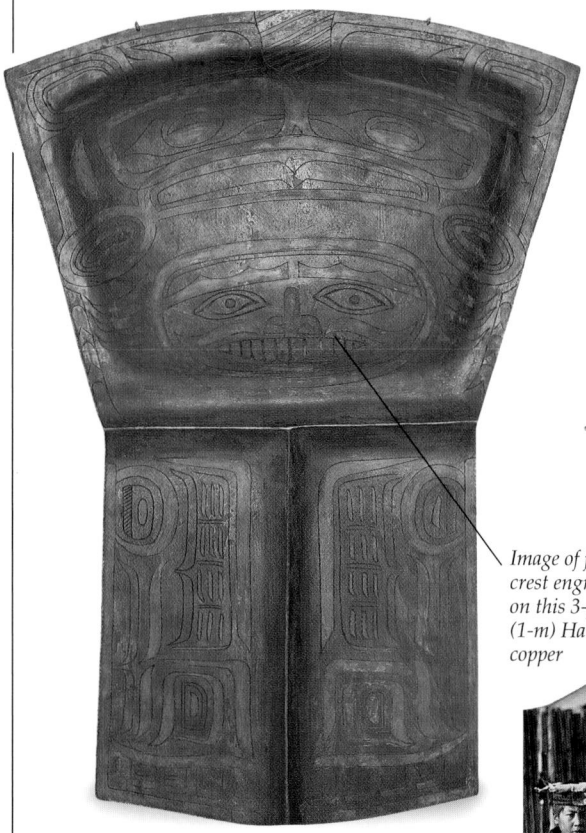

Image of family crest engraved on this 3-ft-high (1-m) Haida copper

MOST PRECIOUS POSSESSION
Shield-shaped plaques of engraved metal, called coppers, were immensely valuable and highly prized as potlatch gifts. Although coppers as symbols of wealth were invented by the Northwest Coast tribes before the arrival of the Europeans, they became even more popular during the 19th-century fur trade period because of the tribes' easy access to copper.

Decoration made from sea lion whiskers

Inlaid abalone shell

Carved wooden beaver with dragonfly on its belly

Flicker feather

Luxurious Haida headdress displays wealth of its owner

Ermine pelt

HAIDA HEADDRESS
Much of the artistic activity among Northwest Coast tribes went into creating their magnificent potlatch costumes. In the 1800s the Haida copied headdresses for ceremonial dances from more northern tribes. Such a headdress (above) would have been worn in association with a Chilkat blanket (below).

Chief Tutlidi and son at Fort Rupert in 1894

BESTOWING A COPPER
The gift of a copper demonstrated great wealth and thus earned prestige, honoring both giver and receiver. Alternatively, in a flamboyant gesture a chief might deliberately break a copper; shown at left is a chief giving away a copper in honor of his son and heir. Rivalry between chiefs was often intense, so one might break a copper and give the pieces to his rival. To avoid shame the recipient was instantly expected to break a copper of equal or greater value.

DRESSED FOR A POTLATCH
Chilkat blankets and dancing dresses (right) were highly valued. They were woven from mountain goat's wool and cedar bark by Tlingit women. The weavers were paid a high fee, so possession of such objects showed the owner's wealth. The dresses were passed on to relatives and were ostentatiously displayed at potlatches, where a host honored his guests by giving them pieces cut from his dress.

A CEREMONIAL HAT
Potlatches were held to celebrate the marriage of a chief, to inaugurate a new clan house, or to mark the death of an old chief. The chief of a household was responsible for managing its harvest from sea and forest (from which he took a share) and for managing relations with other households. At potlatches a host, wearing ceremonial hat (left) and costume, had help from a speaker, who made the formal announcements, and from a master of ceremonies, who also invited the many guests.

WHAT A FEAST!
Potlatches were accompanied by a spectacular feast that might last up to 12 days. The host tried to provide more food than could be eaten by his guests. They paid respect by eating until they were sick. Food included seal meat, fish, berries, and vegetables served with fish oil in feast dishes like this large bear-shaped vessel.

A WORK OF ART
Feast dishes were elaborately carved works of art, part of the visible symbols of a household's rank and wealth. The largest, which could be the size (and shape) of a small canoe, were placed in front of the guest chiefs, who ate from them using spoons of mountain goat horn or wood. Ordinary guests had their food ladled into smaller dishes (above).

Northern hunters

Map of North America showing the Subarctic region

LIFE IN THE SUBARCTIC demanded extraordinary ingenuity, courage, and self-reliance. Summers were short and winters ferocious in the far northern forests and on the tundra. In this hard land, the search for food dominated life. All 30 Subarctic tribes survived by hunting and fishing, adapting to a nomadic life. The Chipewyan depended on caribou and followed the great herds on their seasonal migrations. The Ojibwa were forest hunters, moving between summer and winter camps. The Naskapi of the taiga (coniferous forests) relied on caribou and all kinds of game, like moose and beaver. Meat and fish were preserved by sun-drying or smoking. Hallmarks of the region were wigwams, snowshoes, the birchbark canoe, and skin clothing.

Hood on Ojibwa child's winter coat protects face from severe cold and wind

Hide fastening

Strips of rabbit skin woven together

WARM WINTER WRAP
Winter clothing, generally made of tanned caribou skins with hair side inward, consisted of coats, mittens, leggings or trousers, moccasins, and hoods. Children sometimes wore winter coats woven from strips of rabbit skin. There were big differences between Eastern and Western tribes in styles of decoration. For example, Easterners painted unique red designs on their coats, while Far Westerners used porcupine quills, shells, and beads.

A CHARMED HEAD
Though hunted, bears were regarded with awe by the Subarctic peoples, who believed they possessed powerful spirits. Skulls were thought to retain the bear's spirit and were kept as charms. A hunter would always pray to apologize to a bear's spirit, explaining his need for food and to ask for future successful hunts.

Simple decoration on skull denoted a special honor to bear's spirit

Beaded decoration shows European influence

Strap made of plaited yarn

Slavey tobacco pouch

A BEAR-FUR BAG
Spirits (both good and evil) were soothed through prayers and offerings of tobacco, the smoke rising to comfort the spirits. Tobacco was important in religious and ceremonial life. It was often presented as an invitation to a ceremony or feast, and a gift of tobacco was accepted by the recipient as a great honor.

Sharp end of caribou bone for scraping away flesh

SKIN DRESSING
Preparing caribou skins was a woman's job, and a long and messy one. Split caribou bones, like this Chipewyan set, were used to remove the hair, if not needed, and to scrape away bits of flesh. Next a soup of rotting caribou brains was rubbed into the skin for a smelly but effective tanning process. After a washing, the skin was stretched on a frame and dried, then pulled and worked by hand until pliable. Last, it was smoked over a fire for a final curing.

Naskapi adult's snowshoe

Netting lashed to frame

MOOSE HUNTING
In this detail of a George Catlin painting the hunter is on snowshoes and is holding a spear. He is gliding easily across a snowdrift in pursuit of a moose. A windy day deadened the sound of the snowshoes, while bright sunlight helped harden the animals' footprints in the snow, making it easier to track them.

Netting was separated by using wooden or bone needles

Hide thongs for tying snowshoe to foot

Rawhide netting often made of moose skin

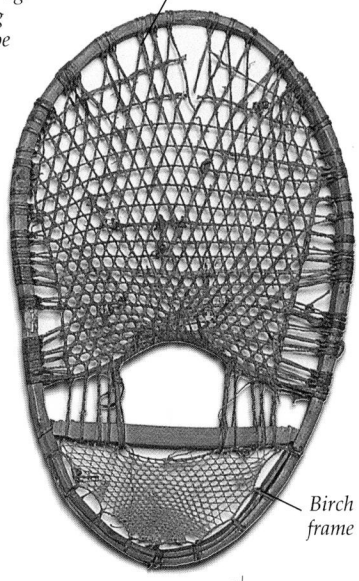

Birch frame

IN DEEP SNOW
Snowshoes allowed the Subarctic peoples to extend their hunting and seasonal migrations into areas otherwise made impassable by deep snow. Moose hunting in winter depended on snowshoes. The hunter could easily follow a moose by its tracks and glide swiftly across the surface of snowdrifts that bogged the moose down.

MAKING A SNOWSHOE
Snowshoe frames were made from a long piece of birch softened and bent with steam, then dried and seasoned. Next, crossbars were slotted into the frame. The netting (called babiche) was cut in continuous strips from rawhide. Shapes developed to meet different sorts of terrain and types of snow. In the Far North, shoes were long and narrow; in the East they were oval or round – as shown in this Cree child's snowshoe.

TRANSPORT BY TOBOGGAN
For transporting goods over snow, toboggans eased the strain on a person's back. Subarctic toboggans were usually made of split-log boards, steam-curled at the front to ride over the snow. They varied in length; some were as long as 8 ft (2.5 m). Toboggans were usually hauled by men, though some tribes, like the Ojibwa, used dogs. The Naskapi despised their long-time enemies, the Inuit, for using dogsleds.

SUMMER ENCAMPMENT ON CANADA'S LAKE HURON
Canadian artist Paul Kane (1810–71) painted an impression of an Ojibwa summer camp (detail above) in the mid-1800s. The Ojibwa left their winter camps in late March to spend the summer fishing, berry picking, harvesting wild rice, and living in birchbark wigwams.

Model of Naskapi man of eastern Canada hauling a toboggan

The frozen Arctic

OUTSIDERS THOUGHT of the Arctic as a terrifying trackless ice-desert, but the Inuit made it their home from Siberia east to Greenland. They lived from the treeless tundra, with its winter temperatures of -50°F (-45°C), to the shores of the Arctic Ocean, which freezes to a depth of 6 ft (2 m). The Inuit thus proved that human beings are the most adaptable of Earth's creatures. They built a way of life on hunting seal, walrus, whale, and caribou. On land they traveled with fast dogsleds. At sea they used skin boats – either one-person kayaks or umiaks, used for killing the largest sea mammals. They developed the world's most efficient cold-weather clothing and housing, fashioning the sturdy igloo from blocks of snow.

Map of North America showing the Arctic region

Bowstring made of twisted sinew

Strips of hide to improve the hand grip

Copper Inuit bow and arrow

Bone foreshaft lashed to shaft with thin strips of sinew

Copper tip

Feather flight

Ivory handle

Steel blade

THE HUNTING SEASONS
Inuit winter camps were on the sea ice where they hunted sea mammals, especially seal. In summer they moved inland to fish and hunt. September was the climax of the summer hunt, when great herds of caribou assembled to migrate south. The Inuit left their summer camps to follow the herds, killing large numbers for food and hides for winter clothing. Favorite hunting techniques were to spear or shoot caribou from kayaks as they swam in small lakes or stampede them into ambushes where they could be shot with arrows at close range.

ALL-PURPOSE KNIFE
Skinning and butchering seals was a woman's task. She used an ulu, a semi-circular knife with a wooden or horn handle. An all-purpose tool, it was also used for scraping skins and in cooking.

Baffin Inuit harpoon

Coiled hide line

Bow drill used to carve ivory cribbage board, c. 1902

Bone mouthpiece

Rawhide bowstring wrapped around shaft

Bow

Wooden shaft rotated by moving the bow

Southampton Inuit bow and arrow

WINTER WALRUS HUNTING
The Inuit hunted walrus to obtain meat for their dogs, hides for boat hulls, and tusks for ivory tools and carvings. One method was to harpoon a walrus at sea from umiaks, let it exhaust itself, then kill it with sharp lances. Walruses were also harpooned while basking on the ice or swimming close to its edge. In ice hunting, the butt of the harpoon was anchored in the ice and the harpoon line fastened at the butt. The harpoon thus became a powerful lever that even a huge walrus could not escape. When the walrus tired, it was drawn in close and lanced.

MAKING FIRE
The Inuit produced fire with the bow drill. It could be used either as a simple drilling tool or for fire making. Spinning the shaft against the base piece made sawdust, which then ignited from the heat generated by the continuing friction.

PERFECT INSULATION
Inuit clothing is light but provides excellent insulation. The hooded anorak is made of animal skins. It is airtight, but it traps a layer of insulating air against the body. Loose at the bottom, it can be ventilated periodically if the wearer starts to perspire by pulling it forward at the neck – hot air escapes upward and cold air enters at the bottom. In kayaks the anoraks were tied around the rim of the manhole to keep water out. Some Inuit wore waterproof anoraks made from seal intestines (right).

ARCTIC SUNGLASSES
Arctic peoples invented sunglasses long before Europeans. Snow and ice glare can cause temporary blindness. Wood or bone goggles, blackened on the inside, blocked most sunlight. Vision was through a horizontal slit.

KEEPING THE SUN OFF
In the summer seal hunts, the Inuit used kayaks – fast, lightweight canoes easily maneuvered by one person. With little or no access to timber, they made the frame of driftwood and covered it with dressed seal skin, which was waterproofed with seal oil. To protect their eyes from the sun's glare off the water and drifting ice floes, hunters wore wooden helmets, often beautifully decorated (right).

CEREMONIAL MASKS
At Inuit rituals male dancers wore wooden face masks representing the spirits of creatures or natural forces, as seen in visions by the shamans. The women wore finger masks (tiny replicas of the men's masks), which focused attention on their flowing hand gestures.

Modern times

THE "VANISHING INDIAN" was how Native North Americans were regarded a century ago. They were expected eventually to join white society or simply die out, but they have refused to do either. Now numbering 2.5 million in the U.S. and Canada, more than half living outside reservations, Native North Americans are reviving tribal traditions and seeking their own role in a multicultural nation. U.S. and Canadian government policy, even when well-meant, tended to make reservations dependent on government support, while tribal resources were plundered by business interests. Despair accompanied unemployment, disease, and lack of education – all far higher than the national average. From the 1970s, militant protests have dramatized key issues but have been less effective than using the law to force compensation for lost rights. Today, many Native peoples hope to bring back traditional forms of decision making and leadership.

WALKING HIGH STEEL
Mohawks of the Northeast are famous for their dangerous and highly skilled work in erecting bridges and skyscrapers. An original twelve, hired in 1886, taught relatives and friends how to "walk the high steel." The 1930s New York skyscraper boom created a Mohawk community that continues to sell its remarkable skills today. Old traditions of bravery and kinship thus operate in a modern industry.

Modern interpretation of traditional Mohawk hairstyle

Coca-Cola bottle on a pedestal

Mohawk spirit motif

MODERN ART
Native North American identity can today inspire an artist but need not dictate subjects. Former high-steel worker Richard Glazer Danay painted this "hard hat" as a modern Mohawk headdress. He mixes sarcastic images of American life, classical art allusions, and motifs echoing Mohawk traditions.

Figure alludes to a Renaissance painting

Modern Mohawk "headdress" painted by Native American artist Richard Glazer Danay in 1982

ANCIENT CEREMONIES
Traditional ceremonies retain force and meaning for the Apache. Dancers (left) wearing symbolic masks, headdresses, and body paint represent Gans (mountain spirit beings). Directed by a shaman, the Gans impersonators perform rituals to gain protection against hostile spirits or to heal the sick. Gans dancers may also provide entertainment at the four-day celebrations marking a girl's coming of age.

Navajo woman baking bread, using traditional oven and equipment

CARRYING ON TRADITIONS
Over 200,000 Navajo live on their 15-million-acre (6-million-ha) reservation, chiefly in Arizona – the largest in the U.S. The Navajo have long been divided over how far to accept white American ways. The tribal council still holds meetings in Navajo, and ceremonies (particularly those for curing illness) remain central to tribal life. Traditional Navajo art, such as weaving and silverwork, is an important source of income.

THE POWER OF POWWOW
Though never abandoned, powwows have again become hugely popular. Nearly a thousand were held in 1993, attended by 90 percent of Native North Americans. They are a way of asserting Native peoples' identity. Many tribes participate in these weekend celebrations focused on dancing. Social dances ("intertribals") are mixed with traditional competition dances.

SOCIAL BENEFITS
Using their rights over their own lands, confirmed by a 1988 Act of Congress, Native Americans have opened gambling casinos in 33 states across the U.S. Casinos provide jobs, and profits pay for housing, schools, and health care. However, arguments over how to spend the money have already divided tribes, and some leaders fear gambling will have bad social effects.

Group of Ojibwa children at a powwow

GETTING AN EDUCATION
Since the 1960s Canadian and U.S. governments have provided funds for new education programs run by the tribes themselves. New schools (teaching in both the tribal language and English) mean that nearly all reservation children now attend school.

NORTHWEST TERRITORIES TRIBAL MEETING
In the 1970s new legal help groups, such as the Native American Rights Fund, won cases before the U.S. Indian Claims Commission. Set up in 1946, it settles land claims arising from broken treaties. The Lakota have received $105 million, and tribes in Maine were awarded $40 million. The Canadian government and the Inuit agreed on a new self-governing Inuit territory (Nunavut) in 1991.

Index

ABC

Anasazi 7, 45–46
Apache 8, 44, 48–50, 63
Arapaho 29, 34
basketry 16–19, 40, 42–44, 49–50, 57
Battle of Little Bighorn 30; Tippecanoe 21
beadwork 8, 11, 13–14, 19, 21, 25–26, 28, 31, 36, 40, 41, 43, 48–49, 58
beans 12, 16, 32, 44, 46, 50
bear claw necklace 22–23
Bella Coola 55
birch bark 12–13, 58–59
Black Hawk 23
Blackfeet 10–11, 28, 34–37
Bodmer, Karl 32–34
bone 7, 9–10, 52, 58, 60
bow and arrow 13–14, 28, 30, 34–36, 38, 40, 52, 60
bow drill 60
buffalo 8–9, 22, 28–33, 36–38, 40
Buffalo Bird Woman 33
bullboat 32
burial 7, 20, 30; mounds 20
canoe 12–13, 53
Catawba 24
Catlin, George 10, 25, 27–28, 33, 59
Cayuga 14–15
ceremonies 10–11, 14–18, 24, 26–27, 29, 32, 34, 36–38, 40, 42–44, 46, 48, 50, 52–58, 61, 63
charms, sacred 13, 41, 58
Cherokee 17, 26
Cheyenne 8, 30, 33
Chickasaw 26
Chilkat 56–57
Chipewyan 58
Choctaw 25–26
chunkey 25
clothing 8, 10–11, 13, 19–21, 26, 30, 38, 40, 48, 51, 58, 60–61
Comanche 35
containers 12, 16–18, 22, 50, 57
copper 56
corn 12, 15–18, 22, 24, 27, 32–33, 44, 46, 50; husk bag 39
Cornplanter 14
cradleboard 31, 41
Crazy Horse 31
Cree 29, 58–59
Creek 26–27
Crow 36
Custer, General 30–31

DEF

Dakota (Sioux) 11, 28, 30–32, 34, 36–37, 63
dances 17, 24–26, 29, 34–36, 42–44, 46–47, 51, 54–57, 61, 63
Datsolali 40
Delaware 18–19
disease 10–11, 15, 43, 54, 62–63
Dog Societies 34
doll 22, 26, 36, 42, 46–47
Eagle Dance 26
education 62–63
Eternal Grandmother 33
Europeans 8–10, 12–14, 18–19, 22, 24–26, 28, 30, 38, 40, 48, 52
False Face Society 15
farming 6, 8–9, 16–17, 20, 22, 24, 26, 28, 32, 40, 42, 44, 48, 50
feathers 8–9, 11, 23, 26, 29, 31, 33–36, 42–43, 45, 47, 51, 56, 60–61
fishing 12, 19, 38, 42, 52, 59–60
fur 8–11, 19, 21, 28, 30–31, 35–36, 49, 57, 61
fur trading 12–14, 16, 31, 38, 49, 56

GHIJ

games 24–25, 27, 29
Geronimo 48
Ghost Dance 34, 40
Grass Dance 29
grave box 52–53; house 52
Great Spirit 18, 36
Green Corn Ceremony 24
Gros Ventre 34
Haida 52–54, 56
Hamatsa 54
Havasupai 44
headdresses 8–9, 31, 33, 36–37, 52, 56–57, 61
Hiawatha 14
Hidatsa 10–11, 32–34
Hohokam 7, 44, 50
Hopewell 20
Hopi 44, 46–50
horn 38–39, 43, 47, 60
horse 8, 15, 18, 25, 28, 31, 32, 35, 39, 45, 48, 50, 51
house, chickee 26; council 27; Natchez 24
housing 7, 14–15, 17–18, 22, 24, 26–29, 32–33, 38, 42, 52, 58–60, 63
hunting 6, 8–9, 12–13, 16, 20–22, 26, 28–30, 32, 38–40, 46, 48, 52, 58–61
Huron 14, 21
Husk Face Society 17, 34, 44
igloo 60
Indian Territory 19, 26
Inuit 9, 60–61, 63
Iroquois 12, 14–18, 21; League 14
Ishi 43
ivory 10, 52, 60–61
jewelry 7, 19–20, 22–23, 26, 48–49, 63
Joseph, Chief 39

KLMN

kachinas 46–47
Kane, Paul 59
kayak 60–61
Keeper of the Smoke 51
Keokuk 23
King Philip 12
Kintpuash 42
kiva 44–45
Kwakiutl 54–56
lacrosse 24–25
language 9, 46, 63; sign 9
lodges, earth 22, 32–33, 38
Longhat, Nellie 19
longhouse 14–15, 17
Madoc 33
Maidu 42–43
Malecite 12–13
Mandan 10, 32–33
maple sugar 16, 22
Martinez, Maria 47
mask 9–10, 15, 17, 46, 51, 54–55, 61
Mato-Tope 33
matrilinear society 15, 46, 49
medicine 10–11, 15, 22–26, 30–31; bag 23; "men" 10, 25, 36
Menominee 22–23
metal 8, 11–12, 14–15, 18–21, 23, 28–29, 31, 48–49, 52–53, 60
Miami 21
Micmac 12
Midewiwin Society 22
migration 6, 8, 28–29, 50, 58–59
Mimbres 7
moccasins 13, 19, 21, 31, 41, 48, 58
Modoc 42; War 42
Mogollon 7
Mohave 42
Mohawk 14, 16, 62
Moyne, Jacques le 9, 17
music 14, 26–27, 37
Naskapi 58–59
Natchez 24
Navajo 7, 44, 48–49, 63
Nez Perce 38–39
Niman 46

OPQ

Ojibwa 16, 22, 30, 58–59, 63
Old Bear 10
Omaha 29, 35
Oneida 14, 16
Onondaga 14
Osceola 27
Paiute 40–41
Paleo-Indians 6
Papago 7, 44, 50–51
parfleche 38
Parker, Quanah 35
Pehriska-Ruhpa 34
pemmican 33
Penobscot 12–13
Pima 7, 44, 50–51
Pocahontas 19
Pomo 42–43
Potawatomi 21–22
potlatch 53, 56–57
pottery 7, 20, 24, 42, 44, 46–47, 49–50
Powhatan 18–19
powwow 63
Pueblo, Bonito 7, 45; San Ildefonso 47; Taos 45
quillwork 28, 31, 42, 58
Quinault 10

RSTU

rattle, turtle-shell 14, 27, 54
reed 22, 34, 39, 40, 50
Remington, Frederic 37
sacred stories 36
saddle 28, 30, 39, 41; bag 31, 39
Sauk and Fox 16, 22–23
Secotan 18
Seminole 26–27
Seneca 14–16
settled villages 8–9, 18, 24, 26–27, 32, 44, 46, 50, 52
shaman 9–11, 21–23, 40, 54
Shawnee 20–21
shell 7, 10, 14, 24–25, 43, 52–58
shinny 29
Sitting Bull 31
skin 10–11, 13, 19, 21, 23, 25, 27–31, 33, 35–38, 38–41, 48–49, 52, 58–61
Slavey 58
Smith, Captain John 19
Snake Ceremonial 44
snow goggles 61; shoes 58–59
soul catcher 10
spirit world 9–11, 13, 15, 17–18, 23, 25, 34, 42, 44, 46, 54–55, 58, 61
squash 12, 16, 22, 32, 44, 46, 50; blossom 46
stomach pusher 10
stone 6, 14, 17–18, 20, 24–25, 27–28, 33, 48, 52
Sun 35, 54–55; Dance 36, 37; Great 24; Mask 55
supernatural power 11, 15, 23, 35–36
Tecumseh 20–21
Temple Mound Builders 24–25
tepee 28–29, 31, 33, 38, 45
Thompson 38–39
Timucua 9, 17
Tlingit 9, 52–54, 57
tobacco 10, 20–21, 23, 49, 53, 58; calumet 34–35; pipe 10–11, 20, 23, 34, 53
Tolowa 43
tools 12–13, 18, 20, 24, 28, 33, 60
totem pole 52–53
travois 28, 31
Tsimshian 10
umiak 60
Ute 40–41
utensils 12, 16–18, 22, 28, 30, 38–39, 57

VWYZ

Viikita 51
Wampanoag 12
wampum 14
war club 14, 34, 39, 48, 52; shield 34–35, 45, 50
War of 1812 12, 21
warfare 8–9, 14, 16, 20–23, 25–26, 29–31, 33–35, 39, 40, 42, 44–45, 48, 50, 52
Washoe 40
weapons 6, 14, 28
weaving 49, 57, 63
White, John 9, 18
wigwam 12, 22, 58–59
wild foods 22, 32, 38–40, 42, 59
Winnebago 9
Winnemucca, Sarah 41
wood 12–15, 17–19, 22, 27, 36–39, 41–42, 49–50, 57, 59; working 9–12, 14–15, 18–19, 22, 24–34, 46–49, 52–57, 59–61
Wounded Knee 34
Wovoka 34, 40
Yahi 43
Yuchi 24–25
Yuman 42
Zuni 44, 46–47, 50

Acknowledgments

Dorling Kindersley would like to thank: The American Museum of Natural History, especially Anibal Rodriguez and Judith Levinson (Anthropology); John Davey (Publications); Deborah Barral, Mark Gostnell, Lize Mogel, Alan Walker, Marco Hernandez, and Rob Muller (Exhibitions); Joe Donato, Tony Macaluso, Martin Daly, Eadwinn Brookes, and Aldwin Phillip (Electricians); Eddy Garcia (Maintenance). Leslie Gerhauser, photographic assistance. Sally Rose, additional research. Helena Spiteri, Tim Button, Sophy D'Angelo, Ivan Finnegan, Kati Poynor, and Susan St. Louis for editorial and design assistance. Dave King and Kate Warren for extra photography, Museum of Mankind.
Artwork: John Woodcock

Picture credits
(t=top b=bottom c=center l=left r=right a=above)
American Indian Contemporary Art: Larry McNeil, 62bl. American Museum of Natural History: 36tl (no. 335493), 43cb (no. 2A342), 52cbr (no. 44309), 56cbr (no. 121545); E.S. Curtis 39tr (no. 335534), 46tl (no. 335553A); J.K. Dixon 28b (no. 316642). Bridgeman Art Library: D.F. Barry, Bismarck, Dakota 31c; British Museum 18c; Private Collection 32c; Royal Ontario Museum, Toronto 59cbr. Trustees of The British Museum: 9cl, 9c. Colorific!/Black Star: J. Cammick 63cl; P.S. Mecca 62r. Comstock: Georg Gerster 45cb. Hutchison Libary: Moser 63br. The Image Bank: Marvin Newman 63tl. Ann Ronan Image Select: 16tr. Collections of the Library of Congress: 30cr. Magnum Photos: E. Arnold 63tr. Mansell Collection: 25cbr, 25b, 49cr. Minnesota Historical Society: 33c. Montana Historical Society, Helena: 34tr. Nevada Historical Society, Reno: 40cra, 41tr. Peter Newark's Western Americana: jacket, 10ca, 10cb, 12ca, 14tl, 19tr, 21br, 23tl, 27cr, 28c, 33tl, 34c, 37bl, 40tl, 46clb. The Arizona Historical Society, Tucson 48tr. Rochester Museum and Science Center, Rochester, NY: (*Formation of the League*, Ernest Smith) 14cr. Royal Ontario Museum, Toronto: (detail from *Hunting Moose Deer in Winter*) 59tr. Service de la Marine, Vincennes: (detail from *Culture & Stationis Ratio*, de Bry) 17br. Smithsonian Institution: Department of Anthropology 30/31 (cat. no. 358425); National Anthropological Archives 19br, 26bc, 27tcr, 30tr, 35tr, 41tl, 42cra, 50cra, 60bcr. Courtesy of The Southwest Museum, Los Angeles: 22c. Frank Spooner Pictures/Gamma: A. Ribeiro 63cr. Trip/Eye Ubiquitous: L Fordyce 63bc. Every effort has been made to trace the copyright holders of photographs. The publishers apologize for any omissions and will amend further editions.

Catalog numbers of artifacts photographed at the AMNH:
1. 50.1/2448. **2.** tl 50.1/1331; tc E/2565; tr 50/3084; cl 50.1/1205; c 50.1/316; CR 60–53; cb 50/3808; bc 50/9789AB. **3.** tl 50/7649; tr 16/902; b 50/5545, 5546. **4.** tl 50/355; tc 50/7388; tr 50/3045; cl 1/2082; clb 50.1/954; bl 50/8405; bc 50/8196; br 50/9485, H/15179. **5.** tr 50/5719. **6.** cl 20.2/2778; tr 20.2/5865, 20.1/8577; c DN/756; br T/2448, 20/6871, T/914, 20/6795. **7.** tl H/5144; tc 29.1/6070; cl H/10426; cr 29.1/7105; bl 29.1/341. **8.** l 50.2/1182A; br 50/9173. **9.** t E/419; br 50/7649. **10.** l 16/4921; cl 50.1/5418; br 16/535, 16.1/769, 16/534. **11.** tl 50/5449A; br 50.1/5466A–H. **12.** tr 50.1/7475; cl 50.1/6443; b 1/4133. **13.** tl 50.2/1320; cr 50/7388; cbr 50.1/7607AB. **14.** l 50.1/1696; ct 50.1/1768. **15.** tl 50.1/1744; r 50.1/1528. **16.** ctr 50.1/5651, 50.1/1544; c 50/3706, 50/6870; bl 50.1/5632A, 50/6188H; br 50.1/5648, 50.1/1852. **17.** tl 50/6486; cr 50.1/1908; bl 50.1/1786, NAE/0064, 50.1/1886. **18.** tr 50.1/1942; cbl 50.1/1943, 50.1/1595; bl 50.1/1603; br 50.1/7572. **19.** tl 50.1/1613AB, 50.1/1614AB. **20.** tr 50.1/6609; cl NN1–4; b T/833. **21.** tl 50.1/8657; tc 50.1/7038; tr 10/34. **22.** tr 50/2232; cl 50.1/7174AB; bl 50/9950, 50/9949, 50/572; br 50.2/1378. **23.** tr 50.1/6625; br 50/4695AB. **24.** cr 50/5336; b 50.1/7215. **25.** tl 20.0/713; tc D/N116; tr 50/5816; ct 50/5363; cb 50/5364. **26.** l 50/3808; tr 50.2/6405, 50.2/6407; c 50/7306. **27.** tl 50/5323. **28.** l 50.1/516, 50.1/507, 508. **29.** tl 50.1/5768AB; cl 50.2/2878; tr 50/311, 50/301A–C. **30.** cl 50.1/7515. **31.** tl 50/5740; bl 50/5756; r 50.1/392, 50.2/6554, 50.1/301, 50.1/323AB, 50.1/8035AB. **32.** l 50.1/5432. **33.** cr 50.1/6012; r 50.1/7894. **34.** cl 1/4606; br 50/5545. **35.** tl 50/5760; br 50/5546. **36.** tr 50/5719; bl 50.1/5652AB; br 50.1/4011A. **37.** tr 50/6166D. **38.** t 16/8648; c 16/8649, 8650A–F; cr 16/9076, 16/9077A; bl 50/3768. **39.** l 16/1285; c 16/8666; br 50/2515. **40.** cb 50/9268; bl 50.2/6786. **41.** l 50.1/5991; cr 50/1275AB; br 50.2/3470AB. **42.** cl 50/3132; bl 1/4681, 4682; r 50/2612. **43.** tl 50/565; tr 50/2588; cr T/18243; br 50/3178, 50/3431, 50.1/2038B. **44.** l 50.1/9232; c 50.2/4760; cr 50.1/4049; b 50.1/9218. **45.** t 50.1/2448. **46.** l 50/9485, H/15179; cl H/15199; tr 50.2/5664; r 50/9523. **47.** tr 50.2/6593; l 50/9433; r 50/9318. **48.** tl 50.2/4817; bl 50/8629; c 50.1/6213AB; cr 50/8405; r 50.1/954. **49.** l 50.2/4819A–D; tr 50.2/4819E; br 50/8196. **50.** tr 50.1/4191; bl 50.1/4776; br 50.1/4889; r 50.1/4182. **51.** c, bl 50.1/4592. **52.** tl E/1525; cl 16/16B; b 16/949. **53.** tr E/806; l 16.1/558B; r 16/8686. **54.** tr, cl 16/6770; cr 16/308; bc E/348; br 19/803. **55.** br 16/1507. **56.** tr 16/245; bl 16.1/404. **57.** l 19/1000; tr 19/1048; c 19/1086; br 19/1239. **58.** tr 50.2/3008; c 50/7028; bl 50.1/7722; br 50/7108, 7109. **59.** tl 50.2/2736B; cr 50/7018B. **60.** l 60/2477, 60/2478A; cl 60.2/5371, 60/6975D; cr 60.1/5361; cb 60/1133–4; br 0/63ABC. **61.** t 60.2/5500; cr 60/5269, 60/3336B, 60/1355; cbr 60.1/3996; b 60.1/3773.